PRAISE FOR NISHA SHARMA'S
THE KARMA MAP

"A heartwarming story about personal growth."

—Kirkus Reviews

"Sharma smartly interlocks . . . classic road-trip novel tropes, capitalizing on the inherent freedom of self-discovery while navigating familial traditions and expectations . . . [and] issues of class, identity, and spirituality."

—Publishers Weekly

"The book wrestles with the spirituality and ritualistic nature of Hinduism and centers the struggles of being a not-here-nor-there diasporic teen."

—Teen Vogue

The Letters We Keep

ALSO BY NISHA SHARMA

Young Adult Romance

My So-Called Bollywood Life

Radha and Jai's Recipe for Romance

The Karma Map

Adult Romance

The Singh Family Trilogy

The Takeover Effect

The Legal Affair

If Shakespeare Were an Auntie Trilogy

Dating Dr. Dil

Tastes Like Shakkar

The Letters We Keep

NISHA SHARMA

SKYSCAPE

Published by Skyscape, New York

www.apub.com

Amazon, the Amazon logo, and Skyscape are trademarks of Amazon.com, Inc., or its affiliates.

ISBN-13: 9781662500732 (hardcover)
ISBN-13: 9781662500749 (paperback)
ISBN-13: 9781662500756 (digital)

Cover illustration and design by Liz Casal
Cover image: © Ninoon / Getty Images

Printed in the United States of America

First edition

This one is for the Desi moms who came to the US and always wanted to go to college but never could. Don't worry, mamas. You raised a generation of strong, resilient, beautiful daughters who carry the torch in your honor.

JANUARY 15, 1972

Dear Jaan,

I still remember the first time we met. In the kaleidoscope room. I was standing at the balcony, and you walked in on the main floor. I looked down just as you looked up at me. There was no music, no gust of wind to flutter our hair. Nothing like the feelings the Bollywood films warned me of in my youth. It was just silence. And in that silence, I was scared. Because I knew our love would be tested until one of us broke.

ONE

Jessie

The Hartceller Bugle

Letter from the dean:

As part of our ongoing commitment to grow Hartceller University into a STEM center of excellence, I'm thrilled to announce that the Buildings Department will begin a one-year restoration project in the Hartceller University Library. After many decades of neglect, we will finally be able to convert the Davidson Tower Reading Room into a state-of-the-art computer and technology center. Our goal is to preserve the architecture and revive it to its former glory prior to the fire damage it sustained in 1972.

J essie Ahuja was attending Hartceller for one reason and one reason only: to become an engineer. Her father had given her the love of taking things apart and putting them back together again, of programming and building something from nothing. And now she was going to make a career out of it.

That was her hope, anyway.

And because there was zero room for failure, she had absolutely no time for parties.

But here she was, the last night of her first-year college orientation, at the Hartceller University South Asian Association get-together. It hadn't even been three days since she moved to campus, and already she was breaking the promise she had made to herself by standing in a frat house decorated like the set of a nineties college sitcom. She should have been studying for her first week of classes, but no.

She was socializing instead.

She scanned the crowd, hoping that no one could tell that she was unenthusiastic about her current predicament. Just like scenes from movies, books, and the random social-media clips that popped up on her feeds, the Alpha Beta Whatever house was poorly lit, with a mismatched collection of curbside furniture and Grandma's basement rejects. There was a TV that took up most of the far wall and a mottled green carpet that needed a good wash. The tables and chairs were a mix of dorm furniture and IKEA finds, and there were paisley and tie-dye tapestries pinned to the wall. A sign welcoming the incoming South Asian students hung across the front windows.

And there were way too many South Asians crammed inside.

At least forty were standing close together in the small living room, and even more were in the kitchen. Jessie was used to seeing this much melanin in one place—she came from a huge Desi community in Houston, Texas—but she'd never seen this many brown people her age gathered together, outside of a wedding.

Realistically, she knew that parties like this happened all the time. But she'd been too busy going to school or working at the family sandwich shop or her friend's father's gas station to attend any.

"This is fun, right?" Tanvi said.

"I mean, I guess."

Tanvi was the one who convinced her to come, and because Jessie liked Tanvi, she hadn't put up too much of a fight. In the three days she'd known her new roommate, she could see Tanvi was a naturally organized and tidy soul, based on her aesthetic desk setup and matching accessories.

More importantly, she was in the fast-track six-year medical program, which meant she was going to be just as busy as Jessie would be.

"It's important to get out and have college experiences," Tanvi said as she pushed her shiny black waves over her shoulder. She braved the drink table to her left, reached into a plastic tub, and pulled out two cans, one of which she handed to Jessie. "We'll be drowning in home-work, labs, and work-study jobs starting tomorrow."

"I just don't see how this is an important experience," Jessie said. She passed the wet can from hand to hand, then wiped her palms against her jeans. She didn't even want to think about the dirty drinks ice-bath water that was now on her clothes.

"We're building our community," Tanvi argued. "And who knows? Maybe someone's rich dad has an internship thing that we could apply for during summer."

"Now you're talking," Jessie said dryly. She tapped her drink against Tanvi's, and they popped their tabs in unison.

She took a sip and pursed her lips. The soda was still lukewarm.

Jessie sighed. At least the South Asian Association had sprung for the name-brand stuff. Someone had told her they had a huge budget for events. Of course, when she considered the small table with two discarded pizza boxes and the soda bucket, she was sure that the upper-class students had used most of the budget for the alcohol they hid in the back for themselves.

"I wonder if Ravi Kumar is going to be here," Tanvi said as she stood on her toes and scanned the living room. She motioned to Jessie's simple V-neck T-shirt and her own corset top. "Not that he would pay us any attention as freshmen."

"Is that someone from your high school?"

Tanvi's eyes went wide. "You're kidding me, right? You don't know Ravi Kumar?"

Jessie took another sip before she spoke. "Guilty."

"His family is *legendary* in the tech industry. His grandfather was on the executive R and D team with Bill Gates, and his father, Neeraj

Kumar, is currently on the board of Bharat Inc., the software company. He created GoGet, the VPN software that all the major corporations use. Then there's Ravi's brother, who launched a start-up when he was still at MIT."

Jessie shrugged. "If his father and brother are the ones who are famous, why do I care about Ravi Kumar?"

"Because he's gorgeous and loaded, and from what I've read, a really nice guy. Everyone on campus seems to love him."

"At least that's something," Jessie said.

She'd be lying if she said that she didn't know about the Kumar legacy. Especially since GoGet was one of the companies that she hoped to one day work for.

There was a loud shout that interrupted her thoughts, and someone held up a speaker over their head from the corner of the living room. Bollywood music began blasting through the house. The heavy drumbeat ricocheted off the paper-thin walls.

And like the cliché they all were, people pushed the rickety coffee table out of the way; the sagging, dingy sofa to the side; and made room for a dance floor.

"Oh my god, I love this song," Tanvi squealed. She gestured toward the group of people who had already filled up the empty space. "This is amazing!"

"Why don't you go dance?" Jessie said.

"Come with me!" She tugged on Jessie's arm.

Jessie shook her head. "The last time I danced was when I had a recital in middle school," she said over the increasing volume. "Look, there are a few people from our orientation session this morning."

The two familiar students were in the middle of the floor, jumping up and down on the bowing hardwood. Jessie couldn't remember what their names were, but she doubted they remembered hers, either.

"Are you sure you don't want to come?" Tanvi asked.

"Absolutely. You can leave your Coke with me if you want."

Tanvi shook her head. "I got it. Thank you!" She then waved at their orientation classmates and gestured if she could dance with them. They motioned her over, and as if she were a fish on a line, she danced through the sea of bodies that had come together in the span of seconds. They waved their hands over their heads and moved to the beat of whatever Bollywood song was playing over the speaker. The air became thick and warm as more and more people began to join, pressing close. Arms were draped over shoulders, and red Solo cups were passed from hand to hand with mysterious purple and brown liquid inside.

Jessie didn't mind staying on the outer perimeter of the crowd. She preferred being left alone; it usually meant she could focus on her work.

But if her parents could see her now, they would be so happy. They always told her she was too serious, and they wanted her to make friends. She wasn't going to tell them that watching them work fourteen-hour days seven days a week was the reason she was determined to work just as hard.

She felt her phone alarm buzz in her back pocket and knew that was her cue to leave. With her part-time job in the student center and her stacked schedule of classes, she needed to get some sleep.

And Tanvi wasn't going to miss her, anyway. There was a group chorus now, and the South Asian Student Association mixer attendees were singing along to the next Bollywood song that she didn't know.

Looking around the room one last time, Jessie heard Hindi blended with Gujarati blended with Punjabi and Urdu and Malayali and Tamil back into English. She was sure there were other languages that she couldn't decipher.

She thought about Tanvi's earlier question. If she was being honest, yeah, this was fun. But she wasn't at Hartceller University to have fun.

"Time to go," she whispered to herself as she took one last sip from her can. She eyed the front door, but there were more people pouring inside, blocking her exit. She turned to the left and found a doorway that led to the kitchen. Bingo.

She motioned to Tanvi and waited until her roommate caught her eye. Then Jessie pointed to the kitchen and waved. Tanvi gave her a thumbs-up and made a "call me" gesture with her hand.

Text me when you get back, she mouthed.

Jessie nodded, then began her journey to the door. She mumbled an *Excuse me* to the two girls who were talking in front of her, then squeezed past another group of upper-class students in deep discussion about a professor. She smelled cologne and perfume, the soft stink of sweat and hair spray. She felt the brush of cotton and satin and synthetic fabric against her skin before she finally reached the kitchen.

There were more drinks here, and towering boxes of pizza that had already been raided and discarded. The few people drinking and standing around the kitchen island cart smiled in her direction, and she did her best to smile back as she reached the squeaky porch door. Without another glance, she pulled it open and stepped outside.

Jessie took a deep breath of the night air, polluted with the light stench of vaping, weed, and booze. There were clusters of people dancing and talking out here, too. She could hear someone laugh in the darkness from somewhere in the yard. There was a fence, and more Greek houses on either side.

Thankfully, no one paid her any attention as she descended the short flight of stairs and walked around the side of the house. She eyed the gate and the dark alley in front of her before she decided to risk the danger factor.

With an obnoxious squeak that could wake the dead, the latch lifted, and she pulled the gate open, stepping cautiously into the shadows. She saw the streetlight in the distance, guiding her toward her destination.

Jessie took two tentative steps before she met a wave of noxious garbage stink and her foot landed perilously close to something that was probably dog poop. "Gross," she muttered under her breath, then kept walking.

Just as she was about to exit the alley and step out onto the front lawn, she ran right into a solid chest.

Jessie stumbled back as she felt the unfamiliar touch of the stranger's hands at her waist. They were strong and firm, with fingers pressing into the softness at her midsection even as the grip kept her on her feet. She recognized his height next. His lean frame was much taller than her five foot five. He also smelled like a heady combination of smoke and cologne. This was different from the scent that permeated the air inside the house. No, this combination was . . . interesting.

"Are you okay?"

She couldn't make out the features of the person talking to her, but they were close enough for her to hear his voice. He had an accent. West Coast. Wealthy boarding- or prep-school education. She had gone to a charter high school on scholarship. She knew the type. Jessie immediately took a step back.

"I'm fine," she said. "Excuse me."

She tried to shift out of the way and cross the lawn, but he blocked her path.

For the first time that night, she felt a trickle of fear. She couldn't see this person because of the shadows, which only caused her heart to beat faster.

"You're not leaving by yourself, are you? Do you have a friend that can walk with you?"

The question sounded sincere, but she wasn't sure if he was just angling to walk her home. The university was like a small city of its own. There were fifteen thousand students, many of whom were housed in multistory buildings throughout the small downtown. Then there were rows of shops, restaurants, and houses that surrounded a train station that had a direct line to New York City. It was unlike Jessie's home in Texas where she had to drive everywhere, but she could manage without help.

"I'm fine. I'm only three blocks up to the left."

She could barely tell by the outline of his shoulders that he'd relaxed. "The freshman dorm tower. I can walk with you if you want. It's not safe at night."

"I'm fine," she said again.

"Okay," he said. Then she heard the familiar click of a vape pen and saw the small red light on the LED screen. When he exhaled, he perfumed the air with a sickeningly sweet scent.

She found it odd that he was standing in the dark alley next to the frat house by himself when most smokers she knew preferred to huddle together in front of buildings where they all talked about their favorite vape flavors and their plans to quit within the next few months.

During the summers when she worked at her friend's father's gas station at night for extra cash, she had become very familiar with the type of kids who vaped and smoked, and she resented how easy it was for them to burn money on something that burned their lungs. Maybe it was bitchy of her to cast judgment over an entire population of people, but she hadn't met anyone who'd proven her wrong.

Before Jessie could stop herself, she blurted out, "You know that's bad for you, right?"

She heard his chuckle and hated that she actually enjoyed the sound. It was deep and complex and held a thousand worldly thoughts that made her feel immature for asking her question.

"Only first-year students are so buttoned-up about vices," he replied, then let out another throaty chuckle. "Don't worry, you'll change. They all do."

"I won't," she said, trying to ignore the low tone of his voice. "At least not when it comes to smoking."

"Vaping."

"Yeah, that's just as bad as smoking. Studies have shown that it's even more addictive."

"I'll keep that in mind," he said, his voice tinged with amusement.

Embarrassment gripped the base of her neck.

Hartceller University was a private institution filled with students whose parents had deep pockets. Most of the South Asians were descended from the first big wave that came into the country in the 1960s and 1970s who had immigrated with starter capital and the time to build wealth. Then there were the immigrant children with rich parents and family they visited regularly in India. They could afford to be here.

Then there were her parents, who immigrated the year she was born out of necessity.

Money and roots set her apart, especially from the person standing in front of her.

"I'm gonna go," she said. She should've just stayed in her room and studied. Now she was just going to dissect every word she'd said for the next two hours before she continued fake arguing with this man in her head.

"That's probably a good idea," he replied.

Her steps faltered. "*Excuse* me?"

In the shadows, she could make out his shrug. "What's the point in staying in a place if you're not going to enjoy yourself?"

"No, it's not that," she said defensively. "I had a good time, but now I'm going to go home. It's my choice." She had no idea why she felt the need to explain herself. She didn't even know this person, but his judgment rubbed her the wrong way.

"Ahh," the stranger said. "A 'pick me' girl. I see it now."

"That's good, because I can't see anything," Jessie said dryly. She crossed her arms over her chest. "And I have no idea what you're talking about."

He took another long drag from his vape pen. "You know, a 'pick me' girl. The kind that thinks they're better than the rest of us South Asians."

"What? I don't think that at all." She didn't know why she was arguing about her character with someone who obviously didn't know anything about her.

"Is the music too Desi for you or something?" he taunted. "The drinking and smoking really that bad? Or is it the fact that we aren't all studying right now and in bed by nine?"

He'd labeled her so efficiently, so accurately, that she backed up a full step. Why did he make her dedication, her commitment sound like such a bad thing? What was the alternative? Failing at her dreams in an effort to fit into a scene that made her feel like an oddball?

There was the sound of conversation behind them, and then the slam of the screen door.

"I have to go," she said again. "I have class then work in the morning." Not that she needed to explain herself, she thought. But it was too late now. The words had come tumbling out of her mouth, as if her thudding heart had a mind of its own.

There was a flicker of red, the richness of smoke, mixed with the musky cologne again. How she noticed his scent over the stink of the garbage in the alley only surprised her.

"You should text your friends," he said. "Or get on the phone with someone. Like I said. This part of town isn't exactly safe to be walking alone at night."

She didn't know what to do with his advice or his alleged concern, but she lifted her phone and waved it in the air as if to show him that she was being safe. The light from her screen illuminated his face, and for the first time, she got a glimpse of the man she'd been talking to.

Perfect bone structure. Thick black brows, and deep brown skin.

"Hey, watch where you're waving that thing," he said, holding up a hand to block her light. "If you wanted to know if I was Ravi Kumar, you could've just asked."

Ravi Kumar.

So this was the tech genius's son. The one that Tanvi had told her about.

He turned his head when someone called his name from the front entrance. "Be right there!" he called out.

Jessie didn't know what else she could say. How was she supposed to act in front of someone that people expected her to respect just because of who he was related to?

Without another word, Jessie sidestepped him and headed toward the street. Then she made a left at the corner onto Main without looking back. She saw her dorm in the distance, two nondescript brown towers next to the student center. With her key-card wallet gripped in one hand and her phone in the other, she quickly made her way up the sidewalk, away from Greek Row.

Her conversation with Ravi Kumar repeated on a loop in her head—just like she knew it would—as she passed empty storefronts, blown-out streetlights, and clusters of strangers leaning against their cars.

There was something about his warning that quickened her pace.

It wasn't until she reached the front of her building that she finally took a deep breath. She scanned her key card next to the door and pulled the handle. That's when she looked over her shoulder. A block back, she made out a figure standing under one of the few working streetlights. Smoke shimmered in a delicate tendril under the yellow glow. The barest hint of a red LED light.

Jessie shook her head. There was no way it was who she thought it could be. She strode into her building, determined to push the memory of the night out of her mind and focus on her first day of college.

TWO

Ravi

Ravi Kumar knew he was a nepo baby: the third generation of a tech family that had amassed enough patents and wealth to keep even his great-grandchildren in luxury. Which meant that he could do whatever the hell he wanted as long as it didn't reflect poorly on his legacy.

There was more than one limitation on his freedom, of course: none of his actions could reflect badly on the family name; he was required to come home during summer breaks and make public appearances during his father's company retreats; and, more importantly, he'd had to fight his parents on the subject of where to go to college. They preferred Harvard or MIT, which was where the men in his family had attended, but he didn't want to follow in anyone's footsteps. No, Ravi wanted to disappear. He wanted an opportunity to pretend that he was fucking normal. And at Hartceller, he had that freedom.

But based on his family's very early morning FaceTime, things were about to change.

"I still have one more year left of school," he said in Hindi.

His father was sitting in his office. A wall of framed awards was positioned behind him in different shapes and sizes, all polished and perfectly displayed to reflect years of service and success in tech innovation, computer science, and math. "We understand that you still have some time, Ravi, but it's good to think about these things now."

"The press is already starting to ask if you are going to follow in your father's footsteps," his mother added. She was holding a chai cup in one hand and her phone in the other. Her hair was freshly washed, and despite not having a stitch of makeup on, she looked as glamorous now as she'd once looked when she graced the big screens in India. Based on the curtain backdrop, she hadn't left the master suite yet and had dialed in from the home office.

"Papa registered his first patent at nineteen," Arjun said. "Our cousins have already launched apps of their own. I'm twenty-six and have my own start-up. You're at an age where you should commit to a career and have an idea of what you want to do."

Ravi barely managed to control his eye roll. Arjun wanted so hard to be the prodigal son that sometimes he ended up sounding like a desperate suck-up instead.

"Dude, did you sleep in your desk chair again? You look like a mess."

Arjun straightened his collar and ran a hand through his spiky hair. "It's 6:00 a.m. here. What do you think?"

"Ravi, we want you to succeed, but we want you to find success on your own path," his father interjected. "A *media studies* major won't help you get an executive position."

"I know what you're saying," Ravi said. He looked at the time on his phone screen, then pushed his chair back. "I don't know why you all called a family meeting to tell me this on my first day of classes, though. Now if you're done, I have to go."

"No, we're not done," his father said. He removed his wire-rimmed glasses and leaned forward. "You're part of a business family. You have a responsibility to hold up our name. You have until winter break to choose an internship with Arjun's or my company; otherwise, we're transferring you to a different school."

Ravi's heart stopped. "I'm not transferring for my senior year of college."

"You will if I say so," he replied calmly. He folded his hands together as if he were delivering a performance evaluation instead of speaking to his son. "It's time for you to get some office or lab experience. Victor will send you a varied list of choices from my office later today. There will be quite a few options that you can choose from."

The name of his father's chief of staff had him straightening in his chair. "Arjun wasn't forced to do an internship!"

"That's because I was winning hackathons at your age," Arjun replied. The smugness in his voice was hard to miss. "I'd already proven myself and committed to a career instead of messing around."

"You're doing an internship," his father repeated. "Nine to five. Winter break, spring break, and through your summer. You'll stop wasting your time with those parties and reading those books that rot your brain—"

Ravi flinched at the reference to his thrillers.

"And if you intentionally sabotage your work, then you *will* be transferred to a different school."

"What if I want to do something outside of the tech sector?" Ravi blurted out. He knew his parents hated his passion for novels, but only because it distracted him from things they thought he should be prioritizing. Honestly, his parents were just as predictable as he probably was.

"*Okay*, I think that's enough for today," his mother interjected, switching to English. She blew him a kiss, as if to soften the tension between Ravi and his father. "Why don't you go to class now, darling? Your father and brother have said what they said, and your brother can help if you want to talk about it."

Ravi didn't even bother saying goodbye as he closed his laptop.

"Damn it," he hissed. He knew that he would have to work eventually, but joining either his father's or his brother's company felt like a death wish. Part of the reason why he was so determined to go to a different school was because he wanted to know if there was anything that excited him as much as tech excited his family. He was good at programming and all the other elements that came with a job in tech, but he didn't like it. There was no soul, no story to the work his family expected him to do. It felt so . . . cold and clinical, when he wanted something different.

He wanted to forge his own path, but now his time was running out.

He tried to shake off the feeling of restraint around his throat before he slipped his computer into his backpack. Today was the first day of class, and as much as people thought he was just dicking around and biding his time before he entered the family enterprise in Silicon Valley, he cared about doing well in his classes. They were a part of his life that he had complete control over, and he wanted to show, even if it was just to himself, that he was good at something other than tech.

Ravi had ten minutes to make the fifteen-minute walk across campus. That meant he'd have to skate there. Maybe the fresh air could help him clear his head.

He shoved aside the stack of paperback thrillers that he had piled on his bedside table to grab the textbook that was buried at the bottom; then he rushed out of his condo. With a wave to the front-door security guard, he hopped on his electric skateboard and cut behind buildings and through parking lots to reach the center of campus. It was still relatively quiet this early in the morning, which meant that he didn't have to worry about crowds to slow him down.

He hopped the curb, passed the food trucks dishing out breakfast burritos to the enamored first-year students standing in line, and strode into the Hart Humanities Building three minutes before the start of class.

Thankfully, he knew exactly where his classroom was and walked right into the lecture hall that fit over one hundred students.

Just as he thought he'd caught his breath, he saw the stranger he'd run into the night before in the alley. He'd followed her home to make sure she got there safely and had memorized her profile, her height, her hair, as the features of the person who fought with him in the darkness. In the bright light of day, he could identify her between one heartbeat and the next.

She sat five rows up from the front, all the way to the left. It was as if he'd conjured her from his dreams. She wore jeans and a T-shirt, similar to her outfit from the night before. Her fingernails were a soft pink, and he was pretty sure that she was the kind of person to paint her toenails to match. She looked up from her tablet, and her gaze met his.

That's when he knew that she recognized him, too. Her eyes went big behind those black square glasses, and her lips parted. He unconsciously started in her direction, as if drawn by an invisible force, before someone shouted his name from the back of the room.

"Ravi," his fraternity brothers called out. He waved, with the intention of stopping next to the first-year girl before heading to the back. His plans were waylaid when Professor Barnard walked in.

"Please take your seats!" she called out as she strode across the front of the lecture hall.

Ravi hesitated for another moment, debating whether or not he should sit next to the freshman. The only problem was that if she wasn't interested and Professor Barnard wanted them to stay in the same seats for the rest of the semester, they'd be stuck together. Then the rest of the semester would go to shit, and he wasn't evil like that. Instead, he walked up the lecture hall stairs toward the very back. He barely finished saying hi before Professor Barnard began talking.

"Welcome to Creative Nonfiction. This class satisfies first-year seminar requirements as well as a humanities credit for English nonmajors. If you look around, you'll see there is an eclectic bunch in here, but my expectations for all of you are the same."

The rustling stopped. The sounds of laptops turning on, bags being shoved under seats was done. There was something about Professor Barnard that commanded everyone's attention. Ravi could respect that. His father was the same way. When Neeraj walked into a room, every person turned and listened. Professor Barnard, with her well-cut beige suit, her hair slicked back in a stately gray bun, and her tanned skin clean of makeup, had everyone holding their breath. She was an institution at the school, and one of the few female professors who had attended Hartceller as an undergrad and graduate student.

"Does anyone know how the university got its name?"

A student on the opposite side of the room raised their hand. They looked familiar to Ravi, but then again, most students wore pajama pants with their hair in topknots at Hartceller.

"Yes," Professor Barnard said, pointing to the student. "Say your name, pronouns, and class."

The student dropped their hand. "My name is Amy, she/they, and I'm a sophomore. The university changed its name from New Jersey Technology Center in the year 2000, after the senator and representative who introduced an immigration reform bill. That's because we became the largest private university in the country for immigrant students."

"That is correct, Amy," Professor Barnard said. "Thank you." She began walking at a slow, measured pace across the front of the classroom. She passed a pen from one hand to the other, pausing to twirl it around her fingertips. "In 1965, the US government signed into law a landmark federal legislation that allowed Southern and Eastern European, African, and Asian immigrants to enter the US for the purposes of employment, family reunification, and asylum. Many immigrants had to come from a specific caste and education status and hold a professional degree, in most circumstances. These restrictions were based on the narrow views of the politicians who signed off on the bipartisan bill. It reeked of colonialism. Of anti-Blackness."

Ravi leaned closer, just as so many of the other students shifted in their seats to listen.

"Then in 1970, Hartceller, then New Jersey Technology Center, started a program to encourage the continued education of immigrant families," Professor Barnard continued. "They welcomed one hundred South Asian students in the first-year undergraduate class. Many of those students had parents who came in the first wave after the immigration reform. Regardless of the biased intentions of our politicians, these students were looking for a new life and an education so they could join the workforce."

Ravi glanced at the back of the new girl's head. He didn't know why he was so curious about her. But he had to wonder how someone her age had gotten to be so uptight. Did she have the same kind of parents he had? Ones that came over decades ago?

"Now some of you may be wondering why we're talking about the origin of the Hartceller University name," Professor Barnard continued. "That's because names have power. They have meaning, and your grade in this class will depend on your interpretation of a name."

Vague, but okay.

"Your final paper in this class will be about your family name, or the name and legacy of someone you value. How did their name develop so much meaning? Why is it important for people to remember?"

A student in the front of the classroom raised their hand. Professor Barnard pointed to them. "Say your name, pronouns, and what class you're in."

"My name is Theo, she/her/hers, and I'm a senior," she said. "Professor Barnard, can we write about the names of people who helped build the university? Like the Davidson family?"

Awareness sparked in Professor Barnard's eyes. "Ahh, yes. The Hartceller Library and the infamous Davidson Tower. I remember all the stories from when I was a student myself. If it's important to you, then yes." She motioned to the room. "Many of you are here because of the name of this institution, but if you all choose to write about the legacy of Davidson Tower, then I'm going to start to question your papers."

A wave of laughter rolled through the classroom. Ravi knew what she was referring to. The two students who disappeared the night of the fire in 1972. Over the years, what had started as a rumor had become campus legend, just like the stories that haunted so many colleges and universities. Hartceller was a young school, but that didn't mean it was exempt from the same type of folklore.

He glanced one more time at the first-year stranger, curious to know if she was interested in the legends and stories that fascinated him, too.

SEPTEMBER 28, 1971

Dear Christian,

I am constantly looking over my shoulder, afraid that someone will know I am not focusing on my studies and writing this letter instead. I fought so hard to obtain admittance to college, to pursue the life that I want for myself. But when you asked if I could write to you, I wasn't able to say no. This is my first letter, but it may also be my last.

THREE

Jessie

H ow was your first shift?" Tanvi asked as she leaned across the U-shaped information desk. Dressed in the cutest coordinated mint-green spandex workout outfit, with her hair tied up in a messy topknot, she had stopped at the student center on her way to the gym.

"It's finished," Jessie said as she got to her feet. She scanned the student-center lobby to make sure that there was no one left who might need to ask her for help.

The space was filled with tables, chairs, couches, pool tables, and a coffee shop directly opposite the information desk. At 5:00 p.m., it was empty.

She felt like she had to be the luckiest work-study student on campus. All she had to do was answer phones, redirect callers to the appropriate department, and hand out maps so people could find their campus building.

In the four hours she'd worked that day, she'd received one call and talked to three first-year students who were asking where the nearest bathrooms were.

"If you're done here, do you want to come to the gym with me?" Tanvi asked. "There's a yoga class that's starting in, like, half an hour."

Jessie used the computer to clock out, then leaned down to lock all the drawers like she'd been trained to do at the start of her shift. "As tempting as that sounds," she said, "I'm going to the library. I had my first comp sci class today, which means lots of lab work. And because I know I'm going to procrastinate, I have to start thinking about my first-year seminar paper, too."

"Oh? Who do you have?"

"Professor Barnard." Jessie picked up her backpack from where she'd tucked it under the desk and looped it over one shoulder. "The majority of our grade is based on an essay about the importance of a name."

Tanvi's eyebrows furrowed. "What does that even mean?"

"It means I'm screwed," she replied. "Especially since it looks like I'm the only student in the class who is struggling with the topic. Everyone else seems to want to write about the Hartceller Library or something."

Tanvi nodded, her topknot bobbing as if agreeing with her. "That's probably because it's haunted. Well, Davidson Tower is haunted."

"*What?*"

"Oh, you didn't hear?" Tanvi twisted her lanyard neck strap around one fist. "There was a fire back in 1972. Apparently, it was an electrical short, but rumor has it that someone set the fire on purpose. Part of the tower was burned. People say that two students were inside, but no bodies were found. You can only access the tower from the basement level of the library now, and they locked it up this semester because they're going to start renovations soon."

Her skin prickled at the back of her neck. "How the heck do you know all of this?" Jessie asked.

"I read it on a message board before I came to campus," Tanvi replied. "There's also a rumor that if you're in the library alone at night, on the basement level, you can hear a woman crying or something."

"Bullshit," Jessie said, even as she fought the urge to shiver. She'd always been fascinated by spooky stories. Watching ghost stories on TV was her way of relaxing after a day of AP classes. That didn't mean she believed every haunting claim on face value, though.

Tanvi held up two fingers. "Swear. I'm just guessing that's probably what the other students in your class want to write about. The no-name student. Anyway, I have to run if I'm going to make that yoga class. You sure you're not up for it?"

"Maybe later this week," Jessie said. "I'll see you in the room tonight, yeah?" She waved at her roommate, then spun on her heels to head toward the back doors so she could cut through the quad toward Hartceller Library. The thought of ghosts and missing persons was intriguing enough that she was tempted to go straight to the basement and see for herself. The anticipation added a bounce to her step.

The library had always been her sanctuary, ever since she was a child. The smell of books; the sensation of running her fingertips over their thick, textured pages; and the hollow silence that enveloped her like a warm blanket were all so comforting and familiar.

As she approached the enormous structure on Davidson Square, built in brick and mortar with curved windows and sharp peaks, she realized that the biggest difference between her library at home and the one on campus was its size. The sheer enormity of Hartceller Library was what dreams were made of.

"Whoa," she whispered to herself as she paused on the sidewalk to take it all in. From this vantage point, she could finally see the whole building in all its glory. There were towers flanking all four corners, the doors were archways, and the windows gleamed in the sunlight. It was at least six stories tall, and in the shape of a rectangle with green lawn on either side.

When she approached the front doors, she was required to scan in using her student badge. She passed a café in the lobby and took the glass elevator to the top floor. Jessie figured she'd save the basement for last and work her way from the top down.

After exploring a temporary exhibit on the top floor featuring books by famous writers that had graduated from the university, she moved on to the next level. When she reached the third floor, she was greeted by a massive circulation desk with a team of people sitting in front of laptops.

By the time Jessie reached the basement, she was buzzing with excitement. Had anyone else in her first-year class come down here to explore? Would her roommate also visit the haunted tower to see if there were ghosts?

When she stepped out of the elevator, the first thing she noticed was the eeriness. There were barely any students, save for a couple near the exit. She also realized that the desks were old and scarred wooden alcoves compared to the white modern lift desks upstairs. The bookshelves hadn't been updated for at least four decades, either, and their industrial metal was coated in a greenish-beige paint. She started walking down the left corridors, then wove through the stacks and the benches.

She stopped when she saw the double doors in the back. Above the doorframe, an old plaque with raised, chipped gold lettering read *Davidson Tower.*

Through the glass, Jessie could see that the lights had been turned off. A long table took up most of the ground-floor level of the tower. There were also chairs covered in white sheets and rolling carts piled high with discarded reference books. She approached the entrance with caution, then looked up to see a balcony on a second level and a gorgeous stretch of stained-glass windows. Just as she made out the image of the scales of justice, a cascade of light filtered through the colored mosaic and cast brilliant warmth on her cheekbones, nose, and eyelids.

It felt like she'd been kissed by magic through a prism. Holding her breath, she clasped the door handle and pulled, only to be confronted by a very solid lock.

The Letters We Keep

"Damn," she murmured.

She turned around, and her gaze landed on the row of study rooms along the left wall. Through their glass walls, she could see they were the only rooms in the basement that looked like they'd been updated with modern tables and chairs. There were even touch screens next to each door to access the booking system.

At night . . . you can hear a woman crying.

She zeroed in on the study room at the end closest to Davidson Tower. There was a chance that she'd be able to see the prism of colors through its glass door.

She crossed the room and tapped on the touch-screen panel. A prompt appeared, requesting her student ID, so she pulled it out of her key-card wallet and scanned it under the red sensor.

The room was apparently available for the rest of the day. She quickly typed in her information to book it. Then, after scanning the basement level behind her, she checked the availability for the rest of the week, blocking off the study times she knew she'd want. She hit enter just as her cell buzzed in her pocket.

"Dad" appeared on the screen.

Jessie entered the study room and closed the door. It smelled of disinfectant and polish, a telltale sign that she was officially the first student to use the space that semester.

Dropping her bag on the table, she answered the call with a smile. "Hello?"

"Hi, bachcha," her father said. "How was your first day of school?"

"Papa, it's not over yet."

"You only had morning classes today, no?"

Jessie paused in the process of unloading her backpack. "How did you know that?"

"When you registered for classes, I stood over your shoulder and took a picture so I knew when not to disturb you when I called."

"Papa," Jessie chided. "You could just ask."

He chuckled. "But then you'll just say, Papa, I'm busy-busy, and I won't know if you're really busy or if you just don't want to talk to your papa."

Jessie rolled her eyes as she took out her laptop that she'd spent all summer working to afford and placed it in front of a chair at the end of the table. Before she sat, she looked through the glass door and saw straight into the enigmatic Davidson Tower.

Perfect.

"Papa," Jessie repeated when her father began rambling. "I promise you that I will always pick up the phone. If I'm busy, I'll call you back right away. Okay?"

"Good," he said, his voice filled with satisfaction. "Now, did you eat? If you had gone to a local school, then you could come home for dinner."

She began spacing out her pens and highlighters in a neat row on the table so that they formed a pastel rainbow, which was exactly how she planned to color-code her reading. "Yes, I ate. And you know this school was the best choice for my future career. All the big companies recruit their engineers at Hartceller."

"There is no sunshine without you here, my bachcha," her father sulked.

She felt a pang of remorse tightening her chest. In the four days she'd been on campus, it wasn't the first time she'd experienced homesickness. "I have a full scholarship here, plus room and board. Even though this school is more expensive than our local university, the fact that I'm going here for free makes it worthwhile. Plus, I'll be done with my master's and my undergrad in five years at this program."

"You already taught yourself everything you need to know," her father said. "And you know business! You've been working at the family store since you were old enough to walk."

Jessie didn't want to tell her father that the franchise sandwich shop in Texas that he'd poured his entire life savings into was not her dream. He'd think that she wasn't proud of the business that had sustained their family since she was a toddler. The truth was exactly the opposite. She was not only proud but humbled by how much her parents had sacrificed for her. But she wanted to do more, be more, and her dreams were now her reality because they were gifts from her parents.

She leaned back to admire her meticulously organized space. "Papa, I'll see you soon," she said. "I promise that everything I'm learning is worthwhile, and I'll tell you all about it the next time I'm home."

She heard him grunt and then make his familiar tsking sound. "It's too far away."

"Now that you know my schedule, we can talk every day until then," she said.

Her father laughed, and with a heartfelt "I love you," they hung up.

Jessie sighed, then opened up her physics book. Under the watchful eye of whatever ghosts lived in the tower, and with the memory of her father's voice in her head, she slid into academic bliss.

She'd barely read through the first chapter of her homework assignment before there was a knock on the door. Ravi Kumar was the last person she expected to see when she looked up, but there he was, staring at her as if she were the ghost of Davidson Tower itself. He wore his hat backward and carried a skateboard under one arm. Even more strange was the look of shock and irritation on his face.

Twice in one day. She knew that he was in her seminar class, but finding him in the library seemed like more than a coincidence.

Jessie got to her feet and opened the door a crack. "Yes?"

"You're in my study room."

She opened the door wider. "Excuse me?"

"I said, you're in my study room." His voice was deeper than she remembered from the previous night, and his words cut through the quiet. "I've been studying in this particular room since I started as a first-year. Five days a week, seven during midterms and finals." He stood with one hand on his backpack strap, and the other on the doorjamb, as if waiting for her to explain herself even though he'd been the one to interrupt her.

"For someone with money and popularity, it sounds like you do an awful lot of unnecessary studying."

His eyebrows jerked, and his jaw set. "You know who I am."

"It's kind of hard not to hear about you from every South Asian on campus."

He nodded, then ran a hand over his scruff. "Okay, so you've made plenty of assumptions about me by now, when I don't even know who you are."

"Jessie. Hi. I checked out the room. There were no other bookings for today." She tapped the screen on the reservation tablet next to the doorframe and then pointed to her name and the time block that appeared seconds later. "See?"

His voice sharpened with frustration. "I've never had to reserve this room in the two years that I've been here."

"Look, I'm sorry that I reserved the room before you and that I blocked it for the rest of the week—"

"For the rest of the week?" He dropped his backpack to the floor and pulled his key card from his wallet. He scanned the card and pulled up the schedule on the tablet. Ravi then scrolled left and right to see the red time blocks. "You have got to be kidding me!"

Was he seriously acting all pissy because of a study room that she'd reserved fair and square? She'd never met someone so entitled. At this point, she felt like she had to stand her ground as a matter of principle. "Sorry," she said, then shrugged. "Better luck next time?"

He propped his hands on his hips, then looked at her table, and then back at Davidson Tower before sizing her up again. "You interested in sharing?"

"The room?" she said, motioning to her pristine setup with her supplies, books, and laptop. "Absolutely not."

"Why?"

"Because I like to study alone," she said. She pointed to the three study rooms along the same side of the wall that were all empty. "You can try one of those. I think they're all free."

She shut the door and enjoyed the look of absolute shock on his face. She had just gotten settled again in her chair when she saw that he scanned his key card and was busy tapping something on the reservation tablet. Then he was gone.

"What did he do?" she murmured. Curiosity got the best of her, and when she couldn't hear anyone, she opened the study-room door again. When she tapped the reservation screen and pulled up the schedule for the week, her jaw dropped.

Ravi Kumar booked the hour before and after her study session for every day that week. Which meant that she couldn't stay longer or come earlier even if she wanted to.

"What an entitled jerk!"

"What was that?"

She whirled to see him leaning against the doorframe of the study room next door. His thick, wavy hair was finger-combed back, and he had a glint in his eye. It was the smirk on his face that pissed her off the most.

Jessie pressed her lips together. "Nothing," she said. "Absolutely nothing." Then she whirled on her heels and strode back into her room. She shut the door with a little more force than she should've, but that didn't matter. There wasn't anyone on their side of the basement level, anyway. She had to focus on physics. That was the priority right now.

Jessie had barely finished all her homework when her time in the study room ended. She knew that it was over because Ravi Kumar, with his terrible taste in music that she heard clearly through the walls, had stopped the thumping EDM and knocked on her door. He'd hitched his backpack over one shoulder with one hand and held up his cell phone to show the time with the other.

She ignored him as she put away her things, sliding her highlighters and pens into their appropriate slots in the front compartment of her ancient Jansport and clipping her laptop into the padded compartment. Then she slid her arms through the straps to secure it against her back and opened the door.

"It's all yours," she said, then turned to walk away.

It was late now, and the basement seemed even eerier than before because night was settling over the library. She wondered how her walk home would be. Her heartbeat accelerated at the thought.

It took her a minute to realize that Ravi was following her to the elevator.

"What are you doing?" she asked as he stepped in line with her. "I thought you had the room now."

"I'll come back," he said.

She pressed the up button on the elevator panel and turned to look at him. He was nearly a foot taller than she was. Now, bathed in the overhead yellow lighting of the library, they could see each other with acute clarity.

"Are you following me?"

Instead of answering, he asked, "Are you going to walk back to your dorm?"

"Maybe. Or the student center to visit the cafeteria. Why?"

"They're both right next to each other," he said with a nod. "I'll walk you. Or we can take the shuttle."

The elevator dinged, and they stepped inside at the same time. Jessie pressed the button for the lobby, then leaned against the wall, her backpack cushioning her from the steel car. "I don't need anyone to walk me. I can go myself."

"You're a first-year, so you don't know the area yet. It's getting late. I'll walk you."

"Ravi, you may be a big deal to other people on campus, but to me—"

"No," he snapped, his words razor sharp. The elevator doors closed even as he stepped back from her. "No, you don't get to judge me, or talk down to me, or make assumptions about who I am because of my last name. If you don't want to talk to me when we walk, that's fine, but I don't want to be the last person who saw you before you got hurt or something."

An uncomfortable sense of shame washed over her, coating her skin like itching powder. "I didn't mean—"

The elevator dinged, and the doors opened. Ravi held out a hand to stop them from closing so that she could exit first.

Even as she rushed through the lobby, she knew that she couldn't escape the truth. Ravi was right. She was judging him and making assumptions. She'd been irritated about the study-room encounter, about how entitled he felt to tell her that the room was his, about how he'd never followed the rules like she had.

But that didn't mean that she could talk down to him for simply being who he was.

Jessie pushed through the double doors of the library entrance and stepped into the balmy September air. It was dusk, and the sky bled from blue to pink.

She turned to face Ravi again. He'd pulled out a vape pen already. "I'll be careful. I'll call my mom or something. You don't have to walk me back—"

"We already went through this," he said.

She huffed, and when he didn't budge, she knew she had no choice but to give in.

"If you're going to insist on playing chaperone, can you wait to do that until I'm inside my building and far away from you?" she said, and pointed to the pen.

He looked down at it then back at her. With a sigh, he shoved it in his back pocket. "Lead the way, Jessie Jaissi Koi Nahin."

She cocked her head. That sounded familiar. Was it the name of a movie? Of a TV show? She couldn't put her finger on it. "Whatever," she said, and cut across the short lawn to the sidewalk that wrapped around Davidson Square and led directly to Main Street.

Jessie could feel Ravi's presence as he walked by her side, but she didn't say anything. She didn't know what to say. In theory, she should apologize, but there had to be a statute of limitations on apologies for stupidity.

Her prayers for a distraction were answered when Ravi's phone began to buzz.

He accepted the call, then pressed the phone to his ear. "Hey, dude, what's up?" he said. "Oh yeah? . . . That sounds cool. I'm in. I have to walk to the student center to check my mail, and then I'll grab an Uber from there and meet you at the restaurant. . . . Yeah, man. . . . Okay. Bye."

She didn't know what to think now. So he wasn't walking her to her dorm because he cared about her safety? Was it just convenient?

He obviously didn't want to tell his friends he was walking a freshman to her dorm. She was a nobody to him, a nobody to his friends, too.

They turned onto Main Street minutes later, and her dorm appeared in the distance next to the student center. Ravi stopped at the corner and pulled his vape pen out of his pocket again.

"See you tomorrow," he said, and waved.

She turned to face him. "Don't you have to go to the student center to check your mail?"

"No," he said.

"But—"

"See you tomorrow," he said again, then took one long, slow suck from his vape pen. It clicked, and the red light on the end of the digital screen lit up.

Jessie couldn't think of a more irritating, more confusing human being than Ravi Kumar. One minute, he was telling her she was in a room he'd claimed for himself, and the next, he was walking her home to ensure her safety. Was his chivalry just some fake act to get people to like him, or was he being genuine? He was a riddle, and she hated how badly she wished she could solve it.

Enough was enough, she thought. Jessie was here to study hard, become an engineer, and make a significant income. Ravi Kumar was occupying more brain space than she ever intended to dedicate to a man.

Without another word, she crossed the street toward her dorm. When she got to the door, she was tempted to turn around and see if he was still there, but she couldn't. No, she refused. Some truths she wasn't willing to find out.

FOUR

Jessie

It had been exactly three weeks since Jessie had started college at Hartceller, and in that time, she learned a few critical things about survival on campus.

The first was to not leave her phone charger unattended, because someone would steal it. The second was to avoid eating any seafood from the dining hall. The third was the hardest pill to swallow. Her arch-nemesis, the man who either took his sweet time leaving her study room or stood around outside her study-room door when her time was up, was the bane of her existence.

Jessie sat across from her roommate, Tanvi, with her salad and Gatorade. "Then after I'm done with all of my sessions, he just walks me back to the dorms in complete silence."

"Every time?" Tanvi asked. She took the top off her burger and squeezed a packet of mayo on the underside of the bun. "Do you guys talk or anything?"

"Nope," Jessie replied. She shook her plastic salad container to distribute the dressing. "He'll stop at the corner of the block and then stand around until I get to the front of the building. When I reach the doors, he pulls out that stupid vape pen and walks away."

"Do you think he likes you?"

Jessie rolled her eyes. The very question of whether someone like Ravi Kumar found someone like her interesting had plagued her for weeks, but like hell she would admit that. She knew that in theory, wanting to spend time with another person was a sign that there was possibly some . . . interest. But she was so different from Ravi.

She didn't have the cash flow to keep up with his fancy lifestyle. The tech gadgets he always had on him, the clothes, or the conversations she overheard about winter break vacations skiing in Colorado or summers in Europe. More importantly, he looked at her like she was a nuisance, an irritation that he had to put up with before he moved on for the rest of his day. "If he liked me, he would let me have the room without trying to fight me for it in the booking portal every week."

"I don't know, maybe that's how rich guys show their affection," Tanvi said before she picked up her burger and took a bite.

"By being irritating? If that's the case, it's not working. Besides, it's . . . I don't know, antifeminist."

Tanvi grinned. "I think it's working. I mean, every time you come back from your study session, all you can talk about is Ravi Kumar this and Ravi Kumar that."

Jessie gasped at the accusation. "I do not!"

"You do too," Tanvi said with a laugh. "And you mention him after your seminar, too."

That was because he decided to move a couple of rows behind her, so now she was constantly aware of his presence. Even worse, his group of friends, who sounded like they were more dedicated to *hanging out* than anything else, moved with him.

"I'm just glad it's the weekend," Jessie said. "I could use a break."

Tanvi snorted as she used a fry to mix together a packet of ketchup and mayo. "Not like that would change anything. You're probably going to spend it studying like you've done for the last two weekends."

"It's cheaper that way." She was saving all her work-study money so she could pay for her flights during winter break. There were also emergency expenses to save up for, like if she got sick or if her computer went on the fritz. She refused to call home and ask her parents to pay for things that she should be able to cover for herself.

Tanvi held out a fry covered in the mayo-ketchup mixture. "I should probably stay in the room this weekend, too. I spent so much money last Saturday when I went out for brunch and for dinner and then to that party. It was like in twelve hours, I spent my budget for the week. My mom is all about enjoying the college experience because her parents never let her. She sent me more money, but I'm sure she'll get tired of that real quick if I do it all the time."

"Ahh, the joys of being a third-generation South Asian kid," Jessie said as she took Tanvi's french fry. She smiled at it ruefully, wondering what it would be like to have disposable income where clothes weren't thrifted and pennies weren't pinched. "Your mother did all of the hard work unpacking generational trauma so you wouldn't have to."

"I'll cheers to that."

A student from their dorm floor walked by their table and waved.

"You know," Tanvi said, her eyes sparkling with mischief. "I heard that Ravi Kumar isn't really big on studying in the first place. That he coasts in all his classes because he doesn't need them. I also heard that this is the first year he's been seen in the library so consistently."

Jessie's stomach clenched. "Oh my god," she whispered as she leaned across the table. "Do you think he's stalking me or something? Am I going to be his next victim?" She was probably being paranoid because she'd been watching too many true-crime shows at night. However, it was better to be prepared than to be taken by surprise.

"You actually think that Ravi Kumar has to resort to stalking?" Tanvi said. She tilted her head back and burst into laughter. "I think most of the population on campus would be willing to sleep with him, and he knows it."

"That's . . . gross."

Tanvi picked up a fry and pointed to the front entrance. "Let's not forget that according to the juniors in my Wednesday yoga class, he has a long-standing hookup relationship with Sahdna."

Jessie turned around to see the direction Tanvi was pointing toward. There was a group of students walking in, and not a single one looked more noticeable than the next. She shifted in her seat to face her roommate again. "I know that I'm going to regret asking, but who is Sahdna?"

"You poor, innocent creature," Tanvi said. "Sahdna is our local makeup and college lifestyle influencer." She wiped a hand against her jeans, then pulled out her phone and opened an app for Jessie to see. "Isn't she stunning?"

A student their age with shiny black hair and perfectly arched brows applied concealer and color corrector under her eyes. Jessie's mouth fell open. "Holy shit, she got rid of those shadows in, like, seconds."

"Uh-huh," Tanvi said, and dropped her phone back on the table.

Jessie turned around and was now able to spot the real-life version of the woman with fantastic under eyes. She was standing at the center of a group by the front entrance. "Now I see her. She's just as pretty in person."

"People say she's going to work at some marketing company when she graduates, because she's already getting job offers. Apparently, she hooked up with Ravi Kumar when they were freshmen, and she's the only girl that he's ever posted on his public profiles."

Jessie twisted in her seat so she could stab her fork in her salad. "How do you have time for classes and for memorizing all of that biology stuff when your head is so full of everything happening on campus? I have no idea how you keep track of it all."

"It's a gift."

Jessie snorted.

Tanvi sat up in her seat, and then nodded in the direction of Sahdna. "Oh look, it's your stalker right now. I guess the rumors were true about those two."

Jessie could feel the hairs on the back of her neck lift. She debated turning around and then cursed under her breath before she looked over her shoulder. Tanvi was right. Ravi and Sahdna now stood side by side, their arms wrapped around each other's waists. They were laughing at something one of their friends had said. Then, as if Ravi could tell that he was being watched, he looked up, and his eyes met Jessie's.

"Shit," she hissed, and quickly looked down at her food.

"Busted," Tanvi said.

"Do you think it's too late to leave?"

"Oh yeah," Tanvi said. "Especially since he and Sahdna are walking in this direction now."

"You're lying," Jessie hissed.

"Not about this I'm not."

Jessie felt her heart speed up, her back go straight as a board. The pesky hairs on the nape of her neck prickled.

"Well, if it isn't Jessie Jaissi Koi Nahin." There was a flutter of laughter from his friends, who had trailed behind him like paparazzi.

Jessie sighed. "Hello, nepo child."

Her words were like a detonation. Not only did his friends stop laughing abruptly, but so did everyone at the nearby tables. She turned to face him and saw that he was the only one wearing a rueful smile.

"What are you doing here?" he asked.

She motioned to her salad. "What most people do in cafeterias." Then she looked at Sahdna, who stood by his side. "Hi. I just saw your video on concealer and color corrector. The one where you use the lipstick and blend with your moisturizer before setting it under concealer. Thanks. I needed to know that."

Sahdna looked like she wasn't sure if she should make friends with someone who was obviously at odds with Ravi. "Uh, thanks."

"Oh, so you're nice to her but not to me?" Ravi asked.

"She's not trying to steal my study room."

"You're the one who stole *my* study room."

Jessie crossed her hands over her chest. "I followed the rules, and I booked the room. You just didn't like that someone else reserved something fair and square and you couldn't get it even after pitching a fit."

His eyebrows furrowed. "I did no such thing."

"There's no way you're in a study room," one of his friends said. He was an unwelcome intrusion in their argument. "This has to be some joke between you two. Ravi and the freshman." His cocked hat was almost as obnoxious as his T-shirt with a marijuana plant on it. He was like a walking cliché and a disaster all at once. "Ravi doesn't need to study. He's a genius! Just like his old man."

"Not quite," Ravi said dryly.

"Ravi, do you study alone?" Sahdna asked as she placed a hand on his chest. "I can always meet you. Then we can get something a bit more private for the two of us."

"Yeah, where is this room, anyway?" a third person asked. They turned to Jessie as if expecting her to rat out their friend.

Jessie saw Ravi's jaw clench.

That's when she realized that he never told anyone when he was in the library. He let his friends, hell, the entire school, believe whatever they wanted about him. She didn't know what he was doing in the room next to hers when they studied side by side, but that didn't seem relevant.

She looked up at his friend and shrugged. "Top floor of the library," she said.

His shoulders visibly relaxed.

"Next time I see you walking in that direction," the boy in the marijuana shirt said to Ravi, "I know exactly where to find you."

"Busted," Ravi replied, chuckling. It was such a hollow and fake sound that Jessie was surprised when no one else seemed to notice.

"Hey, your friend should come to the nineties Bollywood party tonight at the house," the person standing next to Sahdna said as she motioned to Jessie then back at Ravi. "I don't know about you all, but I want to get to know the person who's at odds with our man. Maybe we can all convince her that Ravi isn't such a bad guy. If he's joining the family business, he needs his space."

Jessie almost gagged. How much ass kissing were these people doing? It was almost comical.

"You should come," Sahdna said. She smiled, and it looked sincere. "You and your friend," she said, and motioned to Tanvi. "We were first-year students once, and upper-class students brought us into the fold. It's time we return the favor."

"I don't think—"

"We'll be there," Tanvi said. She rested a hand over Jessie's shoulder and squeezed. "Thanks so much for inviting us."

Jessie looked up at Ravi and wasn't sure how to read his expression. "I have plans and probably shouldn't, but thanks."

"Come," he finally said. His jaw clenched again. "We'll consider it neutral territory. It's the building next door to where we had the South Asian Association mixer. House number thirty-two fifty-eight."

"Ahh," Jessie said. She turned back to her roommate with a pleading expression. Tanvi pressed her palms together like she was begging.

And because there were so many people staring at her and waiting for her response, Jessie had no choice but to say yes.

"Fine," she said. *Talk about peer pressure.*

"Great. See you then," he said.

He winked at Tanvi, who let out a giggle. Ravi then walked away, an arm slung over Sahdna's shoulders. Sahdna waved goodbye over her shoulder before she wrapped her arm around Ravi's waist. Then Jessie and Tanvi were left alone with their lunches.

"Don't say anything," Jessie mumbled.

"Too bad," her roommate replied with a grin. "We're going to an upper-class party!"

JANUARY 10, 1972

Dear Jaan,

Some people might think that my parents didn't want me to go to school. Quite the opposite. They believed in the power of education. But they were worried. We lived in a world that they didn't understand, and they were afraid it would take me away from them. They wanted to make sure that my education would lead me back home.

I'm afraid that you are their greatest fear, and one day I'll have to choose between you and returning to them.

FIVE

Ravi

The last time Ravi was at Amir's frat house for a party, he was a first-year at Hartceller. An hour before the party was set to start, there had been a torrential downpour, and Amir had called in a panic. Their brilliant plan to save the party was to go to Home Depot to buy the biggest tarp they could find along with half a dozen tent poles. They managed to tie the tarp to the gutter and prop it up with the poles, covering a significant portion of the backyard. They even squeezed in three rounds of beer pong before the weight of the tarp pulled the gutter off the house.

As Ravi looked out at the familiar backyard, he spotted a bit of white metal in the corner. Yup, half of the gutter was still broken from that night.

He grinned as the memory replayed in his head, along with a dozen others he'd had with his friends. Ravi loved parties not because of beer pong that resulted in broken gutters like the one in Amir's backyard, but because they gave him the best stories. He enjoyed spending time with people who made him laugh, who gave him memories to tell his friends back home, and who distracted him from reality. He refused to feel guilty for partying, because he planned on collecting as many stories as he possibly could.

Hopefully, the story for that night would include his study-room rival. Ravi doubted she'd stick around for long, though. From the little he knew of her from their brief encounters, it seemed like every bone in her body was serious. He'd noticed the way she meticulously set up her study space and barely left her computer when she sat down to work. He'd also run into her at the information desk in the student center. When she wasn't helping people with a smile on her face, she was engrossed in a textbook.

If he had to guess, Jessie would hold the same drink for an hour, make an excuse and try to slip out the back, and then disregard her safety by walking home alone.

"What's up?" Sahdna asked. She'd been standing by his side, holding a red Solo cup. "You keep looking at the back gate."

"Just wondering if anyone else is going to show up," he said in Hindi. He motioned to the packed yard. "We're going to get shut down if anyone else comes."

Sahdna bumped him in the arm. "Are you sure you weren't keeping an eye out for study-room girl? Your Jessie Jaissi Koi Nahin?"

There is no one like Jessie.

The name of a ridiculous South Asian TV show that was a remake of *Ugly Betty*. Except there was nothing ugly about Jessie. She was beautiful. Her hair was a thick, shiny black waterfall that fell between her shoulder blades. She looked great in whatever she wore, which was usually jeans, white sneakers, and a faded T-shirt with writing on it. His favorites included quotes from Taylor Swift, *Back to the Future*, and a nineties R&B song. They were all probably thrifted. Not that thrifting was a bad thing. At a private university like Hartceller, thrifting was trendy. But to Jessie, it was probably just another way to be practical and save money.

Ravi turned to face Sahdna, the one person he felt like he could talk to honestly about what was going on in his life. "Why are you asking about my study-room rival?"

Sahdna tilted her head to the side, her long, silky hair sliding over her bare shoulders, hanging like a curtain against her black bustier corset. "Because you can't hide anything from me," she replied in Hindi. "Not when we know each other so well."

That was true, he thought as he took her cup and sipped the god-awful beer. Their parents operated in the same circles, which meant that Sahdna was very aware of secrets. She was also the first person he'd hooked up with on campus. It didn't work out, but they'd remained friends. There were too few people in their tiny universe, and it was important to keep the ones he could trust despite their complicated histories.

"She's interesting," Ravi finally said. "She's in my seminar class."

"The gen ed you've been putting off?"

"That's the one," Ravi said, handing back her cup. "She focuses so hard on all the material and takes all these notes. I mean, as far as I can tell from where I'm sitting, she's taking notes. And she has such a regimented study schedule. She is way more serious than anyone I've ever met."

"Even you?" Sahdna asked, raising a brow.

He thought about her question, about all the work he put into his classes. The As that he collected like Pokémon cards. School was something that was solely for him. His exams and papers, all of it was out of his family's control. It was proof that he was good enough to do whatever he wanted. But from what he'd observed of Jessie, he was in the minor leagues. Just from watching her, he could tell that she studied like this was her Hail Mary, her final chance at succeeding. There was no safety net for her, and she knew that with every bone in her body.

"Yes, she most definitely takes college even more seriously than I do."

"Then maybe we should have some fun to help her loosen up, no?"

Ravi was already shaking his head. "Leave the poor first-year girl alone, Sahdna."

"Please," Sahdna said, switching back to English. "I don't play mean-girl games, even though that's what people expect from me. I'm saying you should do some sort of a dare or a gamble. Fight for the study room for the year. See if she's brave enough to take you on and if she wants it that badly. Then you can be rid of her and spend your time with people who are more your speed."

The idea had merit. Only because it would be interesting to see if Jessie was determined enough to play a game with him. But he shook his head.

"If she gets the study room for the year, then I lose out on the little bit of entertainment I have, which is fighting her every Monday to block out the room."

"Irritating me is entertainment?"

Ravi stiffened, then turned to see Jessie and her roommate standing at the edge of the lawn.

"Busted," Sahdna said. She stepped forward and wiggled her fingers in a hello. "I actually don't know your name," she said to Jessie's roommate.

"Tanvi. Nice to meet you." She lifted one hand and wiggled her fingers in a tentative wave.

"Do you want a drink or something?"

Tanvi's eyes brightened. "Yeah, that would be great."

Like the traitor she was, Sahdna winked at Ravi and walked away with Jessie's roommate. That left Jessie and Ravi standing alone at the perimeter of the party. Ravi knew that there were people who were watching out of the corner of their eyes, wondering who the hell Ravi Kumar was talking to. In that moment, he really didn't care. All he could focus on was the fact that Jessie was wearing a dress for the first time in the three weeks that they'd known each other. It fell just below her knees and cinched under her breasts. She still wore the same white sneakers, though. The contrast between the Jessie he knew and the one standing before him was like a magnetic pull that drew him closer to her so he could take in all the details. The way her hair curled at the ends, the graceful lines of her throat, and the soft scent of vanilla.

"You look nice," he said.

She tugged at the hem of the dress. "Thanks. Tanvi made me wear it. She said something about how a nice dress can turn around a bad day."

Ravi motioned to his friend with the universal symbol for drink and then angled his body to hide hers so there was less of a chance that people would interrupt their conversation. "Why are you having a bad day? You didn't have to fight me for the study room. It's the only day when you get it all to yourself."

The corner of her lip quirked. "We got our grades for the first writing assignment in the seminar class. I think the last time I got a C was in elementary school. She hated everything about my piece."

"Ouch. What was it about?"

"Getting into college."

Ravi thought about the assignment and remembered Professor Barnard's comments in his paper. He'd written about a moment when he'd unintentionally made someone cry. "Let me guess," he said. "Not enough emotion?"

"Yes! Why, did you get that, too?"

"Yeah, it was the only feedback she gave me." Professor Barnard had loved the rest of his paper enough to still give him an A.

She leaned back and gave him a skeptical look. "What did you get on the assignment?"

"A pretty decent score," he said. *Great.*

Jessie rolled her eyes. "You're not going to tell me, are you?"

"No," Ravi said, even as he tried to stifle his smile.

"Why not?"

He leaned forward and tugged on the end of her ponytail. Her eyes widened as if in shock, as if she wasn't sure she liked it or was horrified he'd had the audacity to pull her hair in public. "If I tell you the grade, then you're going to assume that I didn't work for it, or you're going to think that grades don't matter to me. Either way, I lose."

Her shoulders relaxed even though she crossed her arms over her chest. "I guess that's fair. I don't mean to, it's just—"

"I'm the son of a tech billionaire, and I'm part of an engineering family. I got it. You're not the first one to question my motives, Jessie. I know I'm privileged. But I earn my grades."

"'Lo," Vik said as he handed a can to Jessie first then to Ravi. Continuing in Hindi, he said, "You're the girl that takes Ravi's study room."

Jessie's expression was one of confusion. "I don't understand Hindi."

"You're South Indian?" Vik asked.

"No, Punjabi."

"Do you speak Punjabi, then?"

"No, my parents spoke English at home. I understand a little bit of it, though."

"Oh," Vik said, nodding. "Biracial."

"Full racial," Jessie replied, her shoulders stiffening. She popped the tab on her drink and took one long gulp. "I'm sorry, what did you say?"

"I asked if you were that girl who's taking Ravi's study room," Vik said.

Jessie glanced at Ravi, then nodded.

Vik faltered, as if he was confused Jessie wasn't defending herself. Ravi had to hide his grin.

"We're just so surprised that anyone would have a beef with our man Ravi," Vik said smoothly. "He's like Mr. Nice Guy. Everyone loves him. Even those who don't speak Hindi."

"Vik," Ravi said sharply.

"What? I'm just *saying*." He looked Jessie up and down as if he couldn't understand why someone who didn't speak Hindi was at the party. Ravi hated when Vik acted like an elitist prick. He, like so many other South Asians at the school, believed language fluency was what made someone sufficiently South Asian, which was such a bullshit barometer. He almost told Vik to cut it out when Jessie responded to his question.

"I booked the room fair and square," Jessie said. "I'm not taking anyone's study room." She turned to Ravi. "Is that what you were talking about before I showed up?"

Ravi took a sip of his beer. "Yeah. Sahdna was suggesting that we do some sort of a challenge to fight for the study room for the rest of the year. Winner takes all."

The last thing Ravi expected was for Jessie's eyes to light up. "You mean you wouldn't book the study room again? I don't have to get up at 6:00 a.m. just to make sure that my time slots are in?"

"I mean, that's the idea of a challenge, but I don't really think—"

"I think that's a great idea!" Vik said. "Hey, guys!" He motioned to a group of friends standing next to the back door near a keg and a table filled with pizza boxes. "Ravi and the freshman are going to do a challenge to fight for their study room. They're going to do a nerd-fight smackdown!"

Ah shit.

"There is no challenge," Ravi called out, hand in the air.

"If this is for a study room in the library," Deep said from the growing crowd, "we should go through the back even though the library is still open. I still have the keys from work. Security and cameras don't cover the employee entrance."

Ravi looked down at Jessie. "Just ignore them," he said.

"As long as I don't get in trouble, I'm game. I just won't do anything that could jeopardize my scholarship."

"The freshman is game!" Vik shouted. There was more cheering.

Another voice called out, "They should go in Davidson Tower! Whoever stays inside the longest wins."

A hush swept over the crowd, and someone said, "Shit, that's haunted."

Ravi watched in surprise as Jessie nodded along.

"Have you heard about the legend of Davidson Tower, freshman?" Vik asked.

"Of course," she said. "There was a fire, and rumors about people being inside even though there were no bodies found."

Vik leaned in close to her face, wiggling his fingers as he spoke. "It's more than that. Apparently, an *Indian* woman set the fire. She fell in love with the son of someone who worked in the university. But she was caught in an embrace with her lover by someone she trusted. That person told her parents, and being the traditional Indian family they were, they reacted by arranging her marriage to someone back in India. But the night before they were going to pick her up from the university, she sneaked into the tower and set fire to it with her lover inside. Neither of them were ever found."

"It's just a stupid legend," Ravi said, interrupting Vik's dramatics. It was always so jarring to hear that the woman who died was a Desi immigrant. He felt a connection to her that he wasn't sure why he felt in the first place. And now, when he looked down at Jessie's curious expression, he felt his heart beat faster. "It's a ghost story that some auntie or uncle probably made up to get their kids to focus on schoolwork instead of dating."

"I have grandparents who went to Hartceller who said that the story is real," someone called out from the back of the crowd.

"I'm willing to spend some time with ghosts," Jessie said, her voice cool and amused, as if she didn't believe in ghost stories at all. She turned to Ravi and stuck out her hand to shake. "Deal?"

His phone buzzed. "No deal."

"Fine," she said, and dropped her hand. "Then I get the study room."

"No, that's not going to—" His phone buzzed again. He looked down at the screen and saw that it was his father's chief of staff. Victor never called unless there was an emergency.

"I have to take this," he said. Ravi gave Jessie a pointed look. "No deal."

Even as he pressed the phone to his ear, his friends were shouting to everyone, "To the library for the first ever Hartceller nerd smackdown!"

He moved away from the crowd. "Hello?"

"I see that you're studying hard," Victor said, his voice droll.

"It's a Friday night," he said. "Is everything okay, Victor?"

"I'm calling to find out why you have declined all three meeting invites I sent you to discuss your internship options."

"You're seriously calling me this late on a Friday night to discuss *work*?" Ravi almost hung up on the man. His obsession with making money for someone else was terrifying. He was afraid he'd be expected to do the same for his father. Just waste away in an office.

"It's important to your family that you start to develop a sense of direction," Victor replied. "You haven't shown any aptitude for—"

"I'm literally the top of my class," he snapped.

"In *media studies*," Victor replied with disdain. "With a minor in *genre fiction*. I don't know what's worse."

Ravi closed his eyes and listened as Victor gave him the same speech his father and brother had given him. It seemed like everyone these days was telling him exactly what he was responsible for, and no one cared what he wanted.

He let Victor ramble for almost five minutes before he realized that the yard was quiet. He turned around and saw that the once-happening party was now an empty relic of cans, cups, and pizza. Where did everyone go?

"Victor," he said, interrupting the speech on an opening in the R and D department. "I'll talk to you later. Please don't call unless someone is dying or filing for divorce."

He hung up, then jogged up the stairs and into the house. Sahdna and Tanvi were in the kitchen, standing close together, speaking quietly to each other. "Where did they go?"

Tanvi looked up, her smile slipping. "Hey, aren't you supposed to be at the library with Jessie?"

"Is that where they went?" He looked at Sahdna and put his full can down on the island. "They have this stupid challenge, and Jessie just went along with them?"

"She's very competitive," Tanvi said, nodding like a bobblehead. Her cheeks were flushed, her eyes bright as she motioned to the door. "My roommate always feels like she has something to prove. I love that about her, though. It makes me want to be better myself."

"Shit." He turned, then raced out the door and jumped down the steps. The library was only two blocks away from the house, so he made quick work sprinting across the courtyard. When he made it to the front of the library, two of the guys who were at the party were vaping out front.

"Where are they?" he asked.

One of them pointed around the side of the building.

Ravi didn't waste any time. He cut through the grass, jumped the retaining wall, and jogged across the empty parking lot until he reached the service entrance. He'd only ever seen it when he was in one of the humanities buildings that faced the rear of the library. Just as he reached the door, his group of friends came out laughing and shushing each other like drunk fools. For god's sake, it was only ten o'clock.

He scanned the crowd and saw that Jessie was missing.

"Where is she?" he asked, his voice hardening.

Vik giggled. "Man, I bet you she's going to piss herself."

"What are you talking about?"

"We thought it would be funny if we locked her in there," Deep said. He was grinning as he shut the service door with a loud click. "The guard will be down there within the hour, but by then, she'll be so scared she's going to stay away from you, brother."

If he punched someone, he knew that it would be all over campus in minutes. But his heart was pounding so hard that he knew he just might take the risk. "Give me the card," he said evenly.

"We can't do that—"

"Give me the key card!" he roared.

Deep startled, probably because Ravi had never yelled at anyone before. He tossed him the lanyard with a set of metal keys and a key card on the end. The crowd was quiet now.

"Get the fuck out," he said to them all. He'd worked so hard to maintain an image of easygoing friendliness, but right at this moment, he couldn't give a shit what people thought about him.

"Dude, we were just having a little fun," Vik said. He scoffed. "I mean, she's a nobody who probably has a thing for you like every other woman who—"

"Don't ever talk about her like that again."

Vik's mouth fell open. "Ravi, what the hell, man?"

"You have no idea who she is," he said, as he tried to reign in his anger. "Look, just go back to the party."

He didn't wait for Vik or the rest of them to reply. Instead, he side-stepped the group, scanned the badge on the service exit, and yanked the door open. He was down the stairwell and into the bottom level of the library in half a minute. Even though it was dark with only the recessed lights to guide the way, he was able to make it to the doors of Davidson Tower within a minute.

Ravi's heart began to race when he didn't see Jessie through the glass. He almost expected her to be waiting for him, with tears and panic in her eyes. Instead, there was no one standing on the other side of the doors. He slapped the key card over the sensor to the far right of the doors and yanked it open. There was a whoosh, almost as if he had released a pressure chamber.

"Jessie!" he shouted, his voice echoing through the multiple stories of dust and doom. "Jessie!"

DECEMBER 2, 1971

Dear Jaan,

I found a place to hide our letters. I've stolen my father's pocketknife, and with some creativity, I've hollowed out a book and placed it in the kaleidoscope room for you to find. Guess which one it is?

Hint: I read it to you in Sanskrit. It's one of the few books I brought with me from India.

SIX

Jessie

When Jessie had first stepped into the library with a group of strange men, she knew right away that she had bit off more than she could chew. But the thought of not having to deal with Ravi Kumar again was so tempting that she said yes to this ridiculous dare. Ravi made her anxious. She felt her pulse race whenever he was near, and she was . . . distracted. If doing a nerd-smackdown dare would get him off her back and out of her mind, then she'd do it. After it was over, she'd be able to focus on what was important.

That was her theory, anyway.

"How long am I supposed to stay in here?" she asked the group of spectators who held open the double doors.

The one who had delivered her beer said, "Let's start with five minutes."

"Okay," she said. She stood on her toes to see if she could spot Ravi in the back.

"He's probably outside finishing his phone call," the guy with the key card said. He tossed it back and forth, smacking the metal keys against the plastic card in his palm. "Don't worry. He'll be here in a minute. Why don't you go inside, and we'll start the clock?"

She looked through the doors into the darkness. The only light came from the stained-glass windows on the second floor. The long table in the center of the bottom floor was covered in dust, and the armchairs in the corner had white sheets draped over them. The balcony from the loft level was dark. In the shadows, she could see old cardboard boxes stacked in corners.

"Come on, freshman," one of the guys said from the back. "Are you committed to holding your ground as master nerd, or are you going to let Ravi win?"

"Hey," she snapped. "I will always be master nerd regardless of the study-room status."

A few of them laughed.

"Well?" Vik said. He reached out a hesitant hand to pat her on the shoulder. "Go on in. We'll shut the door and stand here waiting for you to finish."

Ever since he had given her a drink at the party, she'd had a bad feeling about this guy. His hair was slicked back and shiny with gel. He wore two polo shirts with both collars popped up at his throat. Why did he need to wear two polo shirts in the first place?

"Fine," she said. "Someone start the clock."

The guy standing next to Vik held up his phone with the timer on it. "Ready," he said.

Jessie took a deep breath and stepped into Davidson Tower for the first time. The air felt noticeably colder despite the warm early fall night. It was also quieter than the rest of the basement. She could no longer hear the hum of the air conditioning, the whir of the computers, or the soft tick of the wall clock inside the main library.

Before she could turn around, someone shut the door behind her. Then there was a series of laughter noises and the noticeable click of a lock.

Shit, shit, shit.

"Guys!" she called out. "That's not funny!"

The strangers who she'd come into the library with were already gone when she tried to open the doors. She pushed hard on the metal bar, but there was no give. Her heart began to pound as she realized way too late that she was stuck in Davidson Tower.

"Great," she said. Jessie faced the reading room and squared her shoulders. The light through the windows didn't cast the same warm glow that she was used to seeing during the day. Then she looked up at the turret-shaped ceiling, and her breath caught in her throat. It was like a kaleidoscope of color. She'd never been able to see the intricate design from the doors.

Jessie turned in a slow circle, staring up at the ceiling, and her fear faded like a negligible bruise that was in the back of her mind but no longer something that consumed her thoughts.

She believed in ghosts. She wasn't going to deny it. But she refused to be afraid here in this beautiful tower. If the legend was true and an Indian woman had died here, then Jessie would be respectful in this space.

And if it wasn't true? Well, she'd still appreciate the legends the tower inspired on campus.

Jessie scanned the walls on either side of the door to check for a light switch, but she couldn't find one. She turned on the flashlight on her phone. According to Vik and his friends, who had filled her in on the story, the fire had taken out half of the reading room and a portion of the basement level of the library, but by the next year, 1973, the administration had repaired most of the damage. Since then, very few students had used the tower, so the staff began to use the space for much-needed storage as they shifted into the digital age.

She would love to see if some of the furniture and books were still here from before the fire.

Jessie walked farther into the tower and then took a slow lap around the long table, separating herself from the tower doors. Her heart was still pounding, and she was aware of every single creak and whisper of noise. Her fingers trembled when she pulled back one of the sheets to reveal a gorgeous brown leather armchair.

"Wow," she whispered. The sound echoed around her, filling all the dark spaces.

Then she reached the iron railing of the spiral stairs leading up to the balcony. The boxes she'd seen in the shadows might have some interesting history. Jessie wondered if they contained books predating the fire.

"Just do it," she said aloud to the empty tower room. "Just go up there like the strong, capable woman you are."

Her pep talk needed work, but that didn't dampen her determination. She squared her shoulders again and ascended the spiral staircase to the second level. Her sneakered feet squeaked against the metal.

When she reached the top, she immediately saw a wide, squat desk taking up half the loft space. At least that's what it looked like under the covering. Behind the desk were the boxes stacked and covered in dust. They formed a wall, and each one had a faded label on the front. Jessie moved closer and flashed her phone over the labels.

"Oh my god."

1999.

1982.

1979.

1972.

That was the year of the fire. Jessie looked down at the doors to Davidson Tower, then back at the wall of books. This was probably her only chance.

She quickly moved the stacks of boxes until she got to the one she wanted at the bottom. Then she tugged the sheet off the desk to reveal a beautiful mahogany surface. On the left side, there was a dark burn mark that was dry and brittle, but the rest of it was perfectly intact. This was what the old desks in the library must've looked like, she thought as she put the box on top of it.

Just as she tore off the tape and lifted the flaps, there was a sound of banging from the bottom level as the doors flew open.

"Jessie! Jessie! Are you here?"

Jessie leaned over the balcony railing and waved. "I'm up here. There's no need to shout."

Ravi stood on the bottom floor, staring up at her.

There was a flutter. Some sort of a breeze probably from one of the vents in the ceiling.

"What are you doing?" he called out.

"I'm trying to win a competition for our study room, but I feel like your friends were just messing with me," she replied.

Even in the dim light, she could see the look of astonishment on his face. "Are you seriously calm right now after they locked you in here?"

"Someone was going to find me eventually." She didn't tell him that she thought he'd come to get her before any security could. There was no point in feeding his ego.

He held up a lanyard with a key card at the end. "I'm here to let you out. Come on."

"I need a minute," she said, then turned back to the box on the uncovered table.

Not wasting any more time and appreciating the fact that there was someone else in the tower with her, she pushed the box flaps back, then lifted her phone to better inspect the contents.

There were books, but not the normal reference kind that you would find in a university library. These were romance novels. Hardbacks of Jane Austen, Charlotte Brontë, and even an old, faded copy of a historical romance with the clinch cover.

"What are you doing?" Ravi asked.

Jessie hadn't even realized that he'd come up the stairs to stand over her. "This box is from the year the tower caught fire. I was curious to see if there was anything in here that would tell me about the legend. If it's real or fake."

"You're insane if you think you'll find something that someone already hasn't after *fifty years*. Jessie, who are you?"

She looked up and realized for the first time that his face was masked in anger. "What do you mean?"

He shoved his fingers through his hair. "I mean, what kind of person agrees to go with a strange group of guys to a library, and agrees to walk into the most haunted place on campus without a single iota of common sense?"

Jessie picked up the copy of *Persuasion* that sat at the top of the box and hugged it to her chest. "I don't know why you're *judging* me right now."

"Oh, what, the same way you judge me?"

She leaned back as if his words had struck her silent. Her instinct was to say no. She wanted to disagree with him on principle, but the truth was that he wasn't entirely wrong. She'd assumed he was a prick from the first moment she knew who he was. He hadn't helped change her opinion, of course, but her judgment was fully formed without his help.

"Look, it matters to me that I do well in college, okay? I don't have any backup options or safety net like you do. Working in the same place at the same time helps me do well."

She watched the frustration play across his face, the agitation in every ridged line of his body, as he shoved his fingers through his hair. "It's just a stupid study room!"

"If it was so stupid, then you wouldn't be fighting me for it, would you?" she replied evenly.

"You've had it for a month, and I've had it for two years. Imagine how I feel."

"I don't have to imagine, because time doesn't change the fact that being next to this tower makes me feel like I can focus on my work." Jessie knew she was right. They may not have had anything in common except for their specific quirk to have exactly what they needed in the library.

"Is it so important to you to get your way that you'd put yourself in danger, Jessie?" he asked. His voice softened.

She looked around the space, taking in the silence that blanketed them in secrets. She sighed, her shoulders drooping. "Fine. This was dumb. Coming here with your friends, who are total assholes by the way, wasn't one of my best decisions. But I figured why not? If it means I can be left alone to focus on my work, it's worth it. But I shouldn't have done this."

He held up his hands and took a step back making a clear *you said it, not me* gesture.

"I'm sorry," she said quietly. "Let's go."

She dropped the book into the open box, closed the flaps, and went to put it back on the floor when she bumped into the leg of the table. There was a distinctive pop, and one of its small drawers slid open.

"That's weird," she mused, then went to push it back in, but it jammed.

"What is it?" Ravi asked.

"I don't know," Jessie said. "It's as if there is something behind it and the drawer is stuck." She straightened her dress and, with some maneuvering, got down on her knees, ignoring the dust that was starting to coat her outfit. She tilted her head to look under the table on the side where the scorch marks were visible. Then she heard Ravi pull the drawer open, and a hidden compartment on the back of the drawer dropped.

"Ravi?" she said, her voice high and thin. There was a ringing in her head, telling her that something important was happening. "There's a secret compartment."

"A secret compartment?" He dropped to his hands and knees next to her, his head close to hers as he tried to see under the desk. His shoulder pressed against hers, his scent consuming her senses as he ran a hand over the section that popped out from behind the drawer. It wiggled with the slightest pressure. "Holy shit," he said.

"We have to see what's inside," Jessie said. She turned to look at him, realizing how close their faces were.

He nodded, his breath brushing against her lips. "Let's take the drawer out."

"Okay," Jessie said, and scrambled to her feet. Her heart was pounding harder than it had when she first walked into Davidson Tower.

She ignored Ravi's stare. After taking a deep breath, she gripped the handle and pulled. When it refused to come out of its slot, she wiggled the drawer side to side.

"Here, let me try," Ravi said. He yanked hard on the drawer, then slammed a fist on the surface. The drawer popped out with ease.

"What the hell? How did you do that?"

Ravi put the empty drawer on the desk next to the box. "My grandfather had something like this at his house in India. The drawers always got stuck the same way."

"Good to know," she said. She took her phone and shined its light into the empty cavity. She almost expected to find nothing, but there, under the bright light, lay a book with yellowed and blackened edges.

She swallowed the lump in her throat and reached inside to pull it out. It was a hardcover, just like the ones in the box.

"*Persuasion?*" Ravi said, reading the cover over her shoulder.

"Yes, it's exactly the same as the one I was holding a minute ago, but this one feels different," Jessie said. "Heavier, for some reason." The cover also had a little give in the center. Just as Ravi held his phone up to shine the light down on the book, she slowly opened the cover.

Her breath caught.

"Oh my god," he whispered.

The book was hollowed out, and in the center was a stack of tightly packed letters. *Persuasion* wasn't a thick book, even though the volume she was holding looked like it was bigger than most. There had to be over fifty letters total, and a red ribbon keeping them all together. Jessie took the letters out of their compartment and flipped the stack over to read the front. In the corner on the right-hand side was the date.

March 5, 1972.

Jessie's fingers trembled as she pulled the ribbon to untie the letters. She put the book and the rest of the stack on the desk before she opened the slip of yellowed paper.

Dear Jaan.

Jaan, meaning "life" or "my life" in Hindi.

At the bottom of the letter, in clear black ink, was a signature.
Divya Das.

"Ravi?"

"I see it."

Jessie didn't hesitate. She folded the letter and placed it, along with the rest of the envelopes, inside the book she'd found. With a quick motion, she shoved the drawer back into the desk, and tucked the copy of *Persuasion* securely under one arm.

"Okay," she said. "Now I'm ready to go."

SEVEN

Ravi

The last thing Ravi expected to do at midnight was eat french fries with his new-girl study-room competition, but Jessie had a way of surprising him.

"I've never been here," Jessie said as she bit into another truffle fry. "But then again, I haven't really eaten anywhere other than the campus cafeteria. I've been way too busy with my classes and with work." She clutched the old, faded copy of the Jane Austen novel in one hand as if afraid that once she put it down, their time in Davidson Tower would vanish like a fever dream.

"Why do you think no one found that book after so long?" Ravi asked. He took a sip of his coffee even though he would have preferred vaping. But he knew Jessie didn't like it when he smoked. "All you did was bump it, and you knew right away that something was wrong."

"I don't know," she said with a shrug. "It was obvious from the dust in that room that not many people go in there on a regular basis. Maybe when they moved that desk upstairs, the drawer got jammed? It just needed a bit of a nudge to come loose."

Ravi nodded. "My friend who works in the library—"

"The asshole with the key card that let us in?"

Ravi winced. "Yeah, that one. He said that people are skittish about going back there, but they'll have to by the end of the semester. Once renovations begin, that place will be crawling with construction crew and library staff."

Jessie wiped her hands on the napkin next to her plate, then held out the book with both hands. "There are boxes of books labeled by year. It was only a matter of time before people found the letters in the desk. I think we just got lucky."

Ravi sipped again, then snatched a fry from the plate between them. He had to stop from smiling when color flooded Jessie's cheeks at the intimate action. "Why did you take the book out of the desk? Why not let the secrets stay where they were meant to be for the librarians to discover later?"

Her eyes widened, moving from the fry between his fingers to his face. "We were obviously meant to find these letters first. We now have, I don't know, an obligation, Ravi."

This time, he couldn't hold back the smile.

"Why are you grinning at me?"

"Because I like it when you use my name." It sounded nice, he thought.

She shook her head. "*As I was saying.* We found this for a reason. It's fate. Who knows? I may be able to write about the letters for my final paper in that nonfiction seminar. This woman, because we now know it was a woman, deserves to be named."

Jessie didn't look at him when she spoke. He sat up straight and tilted his head. "Wait a minute. Was all that showmanship in Davidson Tower because you were hoping to find a story for a *class*?"

"Of course not," she said. She looked genuinely affronted by his question. "Everyone is writing about Davidson Tower already. The paper would just be a side benefit. I'm more interested in the love story. Aren't you curious to find out what happened? Don't you want to know if the letters prove whether or not the legend is real?"

"There is one problem," Ravi said, despite his piqued interest. "We don't know if those letters are actually from the person in the legend.

They could be from someone else entirely. And what if they are real? They could be evidence from some missing-person case."

Jessie's face paled. It was as if she was weighing the possibility of jeopardizing her grade against her interest in the letters. He would be lying if he didn't admit that he was also curious to find out what was in them, but a part of him was afraid.

Secrets were more romantic in the shadows than in the light.

The hustle of the diner continued to move around them like a scene from a movie in the sixties while they weighed their options in silence.

Jessie stared down at the book, her fries neglected, her shoulders slumped. "You're right," she said quietly. She put the book down on the table. "We might be able to read them to find out if they're connected to the legend, but I don't want to get into trouble and prevent the truth from coming out."

Okay, so he might not believe in the importance of uncovering secrets, but it was clear that she did. "What are you going to do, then?"

She shrugged. "I feel like we shouldn't just put them back where we found them. Maybe I'll hand them in to the library director in the morning? Say that I found them when I was down near the study room and hope she doesn't get suspicious? Either way, there is no reason for us to spend any more time together than we already have over these, so after today, we can just go about our regular lives—"

"What if I took the fall?" he said. The words rushed from his mouth, as if his heart were afraid his brain would stop him if he waited too long. He was panicking, or at least felt like he was panicking, at the thought of never seeing her again. "If you want to keep the letters to write your paper and find out what happened, I'll tell everyone that it was me who found them. I'm not on scholarship, and because of my family name, I doubt I'd get in trouble. If this means something to you, then I'll help."

"Why?" she blurted out. Her hands rested on the table between them, as if reaching out to understand his motive. "Why would you do that?"

"Because I feel responsible," he said, sharing a half-truth with her. "Because you wouldn't have been locked in there if it wasn't for my dumb friends, and I'm hoping that you're still willing to share the study room after you stayed the longest in Davidson Tower."

She smiled at him, and it softened all her harsh lines and edges. "Because of guilt and a study room, you'd take the fall?"

"Got to use my nepo-baby status for some good, right?" he said ruefully.

"Thanks, but you'd still be paying too high of a price to cover for me."

He thought about it, about their time together and their rush to get the study room after the last few weeks. The idea of not spending any more time with her didn't sit right with him. He'd have to think about why he felt that way later, but in the moment, he knew he didn't want to lose their shared moments of open and honest conversation. With Jessie, he could be himself, and he knew Jessie wouldn't lie to him about her feelings. "I'll tell you what. We can read them together."

"You want to read the letters, too?" she asked, with one perfectly arched brow.

Ravi understood why she had doubts, but he wasn't exactly going to tell her that he was more interested in spending time with *her* than in reading letters. "Yeah," he said. "I have the same class you do. Maybe we can both write about the letters for our final papers."

She nodded. Her hair was up in a messy bun now, and her shoulders were bare. "I mean, wouldn't you want to write about *your* name instead?"

Ravi scoffed. "What's the fun in that? No, this sounds like a way more intriguing story to follow."

"Fine," she said. "We can get together next week and read them all—"

"Nope," he said.

She gaped at him, and he had to hide his smile behind his coffee cup. Her expression was so earnest. "What do you mean, 'nope'?" she blurted.

"Don't you remember what we learned in class, Jessie Jaissi Koi Nahin? What's one of the first rules of writing an observational piece?"

"Pay attention to the details," she recited.

"If we blow through all the letters at once, then we may miss some very important clues." He knew he was making excuses now, but hopefully she'd humor him. "We should read one or two letters at a time, decipher them, and then move on to the next."

She looked down at the book. Her finger ran under the lip of the cover as if she were on the verge of exposing its contents to the diner crowd. There was that huff of air, that admittance of defeat that he heard from her the first time he told her not to judge him for his name. "I guess you're right. Do you mind if I hold on to them, though?"

"No, go for it."

There was that smile again. The one that he liked to see. "You trust that I won't read them without you? That I'll keep our promise?"

He nodded slowly. "I don't know a lot about you, but I have a feeling you're the kind of person who'll stick to their word."

She smiled again. It was the second time that night. "Great."

He crossed his arms and leaned on the table. "Do you want to start now? Reading the letters, I mean."

Jessie shook her head. "I'd rather we do it either in the study room or someplace where there's not that many people."

"Fine," he said. "That works for me."

She bit into another fry, and they slipped into silence as they ate and sipped their drinks in that bustling late-night diner filled with upper-class students who looked like they were desperately trying to sober up. The silence wasn't new between them. After all the times he had walked by her side, Ravi was used to the quiet. It felt comfortable now.

Later that night, after he accompanied her back to her dorm room and watched her carry the hollowed-out book like it was precious cargo cradled in her arms, he took the long way back to his condo. It was on the edge of campus, closer to the downtown district than to any of the university buildings.

His parents had encouraged him to live in the dorms. They believed that he'd learn from his peers and feel challenged to do better. Competition, according to them, was an excellent motivator.

But Ravi knew that meant he'd constantly be living under a microscope. He was hardly able to go a day on campus without someone trying to talk him up or a teacher calling on him, expecting him to know the answer because of who he was. If there was one thing he desperately needed for his sanity after a full day of attention, it was a quiet place where he didn't have to pretend to be what everyone wanted him to be.

That was why Ravi bought the condo in secret. He'd used part of the trust money that he'd been able to access when he turned eighteen. It was meant to pay for college, but he'd gotten merit scholarships. The summer before his first year, he told his family he had to fly out for orientation. He'd used that time to secure a unit in the new-construction high-rise. He lived one level below the penthouse and had two bedrooms and two and a half baths, a balcony that overlooked the downtown area and campus, as well as hardwood floors and state-of-the-art appliances. He had someone come in once a week to clean, and he had prepared meals delivered every Thursday night.

The best part about his place? It was all his.

Ravi waved at the doorman, then took the elevator to his floor, where he pressed his thumb over the fingerprint scanner and entered his quiet condo. It was spotless. The only chaos was colorful, eclectic covers of his favorite paperbacks that he displayed in a rainbow pattern on shelves bracketing his TV. There were stacks of books on the coffee table, the dining table, and the floor next to the sofa, too. He had no other art, no souvenirs or picture frames.

Ravi kicked off his shoes on the doormat next to the entrance and then walked barefoot to his bedroom, stripping off clothes as he went.

Even though it was one in the morning, he strode into his ensuite bathroom and turned on the overhead rain shower before he stepped inside the glass-and-tile enclosure.

Jessie came to mind.

She looked so excited to find the book. It was as if she thought every single letter would have the answer to all her life problems. But the real world wasn't that fantastical, and he knew the reality contained in the letters had the potential of dashing any hopes of a happily ever after he knew Jessie was looking for. That didn't stop memories of her smile or her cutting humor from invading his thoughts. He closed his eyes and stepped under the hot spray. He rested one hand on the tiled wall on front of him as he gave in to the urge to stroke himself at the thought of her.

When he was spent, Ravi turned off the faucet and stepped out of the shower stall, careful not to slip on the wet tile. He pulled on some boxers, grabbed his vape pen, then walked into the guest bedroom that he'd converted into a small office space. He pulled out his high-back leather chair at his desk and sat in front of his computer. His heart swelled as a story began to form. The words were like smoke tendrils, disappearing if he didn't pay close attention.

For the first time since he was a child, when he used to tell stories to his grandfather for fun, Ravi decided to write his own happily ever after. He opened up a blank Word document and focused on the blinking cursor.

"I can't believe I'm doing this," he murmured, then began typing.

EIGHT

Jessie

Jessie had made plans to go to brunch with Tanvi Saturday afternoon right before her shift at the student center. It was the only time she allowed herself to eat off campus outside of her meal plan. She knew that Tanvi would want all the details about what happened after the party, and she'd been dreading the inquisition.

But the gods were on her side today.

"Do you think we can rain check brunch?" Tanvi croaked from under her blanket. "I have the mother of all hangovers."

"Do you want me to get you anything?" Jessie asked as she grabbed her bathroom tote and flip-flops. The room was still dark, their curtains drawn and the lights switched off, even though it was already eleven. "I can run down to the convenience store at the corner and grab some Tylenol and Gatorade."

Tanvi's arms appeared from under the blanket, and she pointed to the fridge that they'd tucked under her lofted bed. "I have one in there. Can you hand it to me?"

Jessie opened their mini fridge, took out the red Gatorade bottle, and tucked it in Tanvi's hand. It disappeared under the blanket. "Thanks."

"No problem," Jessie said. She turned to go, when Tanvi called her name again.

"Don't think I forgot about yesterday," she croaked.

"Right," Jessie said, then left as quickly as she could before the Gatorade really kicked in and the questioning started while she was still in her smiley-face pajama pants.

Jessie didn't expect it to be so difficult to keep a promise. Ravi said he was going to cover for her, and she believed him. Which meant that she had to give him a reason to believe her, too. She entered the bathroom and made quick work of her basic skincare routine and shower ritual. She wasn't washing her hair that day, so she quickly applied some dry shampoo and tied it in a topknot. Maybe she'd get started on homework for her Wednesday classes while she was working her shift at the information desk. She had a quiz she could prepare for, and a coding assignment as well.

"Hey, are you Jessie?"

Jessie turned around from the vanity mirror and table station where she'd been applying sunscreen to look at the two unfamiliar people that had walked into the bathroom. They were both Desi, and Jessie was pretty sure they lived on her floor.

"I am," she said slowly. "Hi."

"Hi!" they said brightly. "We heard that you're Ravi Kumar's study partner, and we—"

"I'm sorry, *what?*"

They looked at each other and then took a step back as if her reaction were completely unreasonable. The one on the left spoke first.

"We heard he's hanging out with a new girl. A first-year Desi named Jessie. And you're the only student named Jessie. There was a picture of you two together last night at a diner. My friend Jason sent it to us. We just wanted to know, is he as nice as people say he is? We're just really curious."

Jessie could feel her heart pounding under their scrutiny. At least they were nice about it. It's not like they shoved their phones at her. "Uh, we're not *together* or anything," she said. "We have a class together.

Seminar. And last night, we were in the same place at the same time, I guess. Anyway. He's polite to freshmen like me."

She saw their hope fade on their faces, as if they had wondered if there was an opportunity for them to have a fairy-tale romance.

The girl on the left motioned to her bathroom tote. "Sorry, I know this seems really weird to catch you like this, but we weren't stalking or anything. We were headed to the dining hall and stopped to go to the bathroom, but then there you were. We heard he got all of his friends jobs over the summer. That's the dream."

Jessie smiled at them. "Yeah, that actually sounds like him." She wasn't sure if it was true or not, but it fit with Ravi's reputation. He was genuinely a nice guy, even though he had his grumpy moments with her.

"Anyway, thanks," the one on the right said. "We'll see you around."

"See you," Jessie said. When they left, she picked up her phone and sent a text to the number she'd added the night before. Well, technically a few hours ago.

JESSIE: People know that we know each other.

A response came seconds later.

RAVI: So?

JESSIE: So . . . I prefer to not draw any attention to myself. People are going to start viewing me as competition or something. Hey, did you really give jobs to all of your friends? And how many girlfriends do you go through?

RAVI: Relax, JJKN. Those are all rumors. No one is going to see you as competition if you don't want them to.

Jessie looked up from her phone. "What the heck is JJKN?" It took her a minute to put the pieces together. *Jessie Jaissi Koi Nahin.* The

Indian remake of *Ugly Betty*. She'd looked it up after the first time he'd called her that ridiculous name.

JESSIE: I guess we'll just have to keep it on the down-low or something. My family believes in the evil eye, and I don't want that to affect my grades.

RAVI: If you're ashamed to be seen with me, it'll be real hard working on our project together. Don't forget, we're reading the letters as a team. Unless you'd rather not?

Jessie looked down at his text and rubbed her fingers against her temple. Shit, she'd offended him.

She shouldn't care. It shouldn't matter. But other than their petty war in the booking system to secure the study room, he'd been . . . fair. He'd walked her home at night every single time she left after dark. He'd given up the room when it was her turn even though he could've been an ass and stayed longer. And he didn't treat her like dirt, like some of the other upper-class students did to the incoming first-years. She typed a quick message and hit send before she could rethink her decision.

JESSIE: I'm sorry. You didn't deserve that.

Three dots popped up, a bubble of anticipation on her screen.

RAVI: Thanks.

Jessie let out a breath. "He'll forgive me," she whispered as she put her phone in her back pocket and packed up her bathroom tote.

That was as much as she could expect in her current circumstances.

JANUARY 30, 1972

Dear Jaan,

I wish I could focus on my studies today, but thoughts of our conversation from last night keep replaying over and over again in my mind. We come from such different places, but we aren't so different after all. Your parents expect just as much from you as mine do from me. But this is where we are different: you have the choice to be someone different. I'll never be anything but what I'm told to be.

NINE

Ravi

Ravi should've walked away from Jessie when he had the chance. He could find another study room, and he could give her the space she obviously was asking for. But it irritated him that she thought his presence could cause something as bad as the "evil eye."

He didn't know what possessed him to go seek her out after class on Monday, but he wanted to talk to her in person. Maybe he needed to hear her say that she didn't want to be seen with him before they met up at the library later.

He tucked his electric skateboard into the elastic straps at the front of his backpack to secure it in place, and he strolled toward the student center.

Anticipation bubbled in his veins even as his phone buzzed with an incoming text. He paused in front of the entrance so he could look down at his screen.

ARJUN: Pick an internship. Victor told me that you blew him off.

How did his family get so good at crawling under his skin? He stopped long enough to text back.

RAVI: He called on a Friday night. And I have time.

ARJUN: No, you don't.

Instead of taking the bait, Ravi shoved his phone back into his pocket. He wasn't going to engage. Not now, when he had more important things to do. Like talking to Jessie.

He yanked open the double doors and strode inside. Students were sitting in the open seating area with textbooks and laptops. The café had a short line and two baristas working the espresso machine and the cash register.

Someone called his name from the back corner. He turned to see a cluster of students from his class. He couldn't remember their names, but he was pretty sure two of them were in one of his media studies lectures. He waved and smiled in their direction before turning forward again.

There was Jessie. She sat behind the information desk, her tablet stylus shoved through the ponytail at the top of her head and her bottom lip worried between her teeth. She had a crease between her eyebrows, a tiny line that he'd noticed when he saw her concentrating on a problem.

Ravi approached the desk and folded his hands on the raised ledge. He leaned forward when she didn't notice him. "Hey," he said. "Can I get some help?"

Jessie jolted in her seat and rolled back half a foot. Her eyes were as wide as saucers, and she pressed a hand against her chest. "Holy cow," she said, gasping for air. "You scared the crap out of me."

"Sorry about that," he said. He couldn't help but smile. "A little jumpy, I see."

"What are you doing here?"

He knew she was going to ask that question, and he still wasn't sure he was willing to tell her the truth about how much her text had affected him. "Why? Are you embarrassed to be seen with me?"

Her face clouded with guilt. "No, that's not what I meant. And . . . I'm, ah, sorry. About what I said."

"Did you mean it?"

She cocked her head to the side. "What?"

"Did you *mean* it?" Ravi asked again. He leaned closer and could see the flecks of gold in her irises. Her bow lips parted. "Are you worried that being seen with me will give you the evil eye or something? Do you think we should meet on the down-low because you don't want people to know that we're . . . acquaintances?"

"The problem is that people think we're more than *acquaintances*," she said as she removed the pencil from her hair. "And no, I didn't mean it about the evil eye. But, Ravi, you have to admit being your friend comes with hefty fees."

She was right. Of course, she was right. Between his family, classmates, and professors who all thought he was going to be the next best thing in STEM, and his own hang-ups about pursuing a career that bored him to tears, Jessie's reasons were completely valid. But he hated knowing that the one person he was able to be himself around was the same person who didn't like what she knew about him.

"You're right," he said slowly. "Fine, do you want me to go?"

She let out a deep breath. "No, it's okay. I mean, you probably should just because I'm at work, but not because of the whole evil-eye thing."

He snorted. The information desk was a dead zone unless it was parents' weekend or something. "Are you serious? I bet you could leave right now for the rest of your shift and it wouldn't matter at all."

Ravi knew he'd said the wrong thing when her back went ramrod straight. "I would *never*," she said. "You may not have to work for your education, but this job means a lot to me."

He thought about his brother's text and the ultimatum about the internship. "Why?"

She blinked owlishly. "Why, what?"

"Why does the job mean a lot to you? Besides the money."

Jessie cocked her head to the side, her brows furrowing. "I guess it's because it gives me the freedom to pay for what I need to so my parents don't have to worry about me."

"So it's more for your parents?" he pressed. Ravi was genuinely curious. Now that he admitted to himself that he had feelings for her, he wanted to know everything about her. All her likes, dislikes, and happy moments from before she stepped into his life. Maybe if he could understand her, he'd understand why he liked her so much, and then he'd understand himself.

Jessie got to her feet, then looked over Ravi's shoulder as if scanning the student center to make sure that no one could hear her next few words. "Ravi, are you okay?"

"What? Yeah, of course. Why?"

"Because you're not acting like the Ravi I know," she said. "Not that I know you very well, but enough to see that you're different. And maybe this is just another side of you I haven't met before, but I don't think so."

He wanted to tell her about the internship. About his parents and brother. She should know about him, too. Maybe that would help her understand him better as well. Instead, he rocked back on his heels. "We should probably figure out a time to meet up and talk about the letters," he said.

Her eyes narrowed again, and that tiny line of concentration formed between her brows. "Yeah, we should."

"I can do tomorrow."

"Me too."

"Great," he said. He knocked twice on the desk, unsure of why he came. Why he needed to see her, to figure her out. "I guess I'll see you around, then."

"Ravi?" She called his name just as he turned to go.

"Yeah?"

"For the record," she said softly. "Sometimes the job really is about the money. Because dreams aren't cheap. Ask anyone whose parents raised them paycheck to paycheck, and they'll tell you."

"Is that why you want to become an engineer?" he said. "Not because you're passionate about it, but because of the money? Because dreaming of anything else is too expensive to risk?"

90

"Partly," she said. "And I'm not ashamed of it, either." She raised her chin. "It's what my father never could do, and it's something that I'm good at and that challenges me."

"And it'll make you happy," Ravi said quietly.

She nodded. Her hands running over the smooth wood of the desk. "Yes," she said. "And it makes me happy. But you have to figure out what works for you. My reasons won't be the same as yours. And yours won't be the same as your friends'. Like . . . Sahdna."

He wanted to laugh, but he knew if he did, it would sound bitter and leave an acrid taste in his mouth. "My father would love it if my goals and my reasons were the same as yours," he said ruefully. "And Sahdna's dreams are the same as my parents', so no, I can't see things the same way she does. I'll see you Tuesday, Jessie Jaissi Koi Nahin," he called out over his shoulder. And then he was pushing through the front doors to step outside. He needed his vape.

TEN

Jessie

Jessie couldn't stop thinking about Ravi's visit for the rest of the day. When it came time to review the letters, she was sure their meeting was going to be just as awkward. Except when he arrived, it was as if they had never spoken about evil eyes or money at all. He strolled into the study room, his easy swagger on full display.

"Hey," Ravi said. He had switched out his usual pair of cargo shorts for jeans and a fitted T-shirt. As casual and worn-in as both of those items looked, Jessie knew they probably cost a fortune. His entire wardrobe was expensive yet unassuming, including the bomber jacket he said was a Balmain vintage. As if she'd know Balmain from Old Navy.

Then there was the backward hat that always had her pulse fluttering.

Damn it, why did she like the backward hat so much?

"Sorry I'm late," he said as he stepped inside and closed the door at his back. The room instantly felt smaller. "I had a call with my parents. They're in Australia right now, so it's hard to get a hold of them."

The question was on the tip of her tongue, but she bit it back. He must've noticed her expression, because he slid his backpack onto the table and dropped into the chair opposite from where she was standing. "Just ask, Jessie."

Her breath came out with a rush. "What was it like?" she said. "What's it like visiting all those places, and having all that money?"

"I don't know," he replied. "Normal?"

"Normal?"

"Normal," Ravi repeated. Then shook his head as if he was unsure whether or not to tell her the truth. He'd been honest with her as far as she knew, but because he was questioning himself now made her wonder what he was hiding. "Jessie, I never went on those trips growing up. At least not until I was a teenager and forced to tag along when my father had a business conference. For the most part, I was at home with my mom, my brother, or my grandparents, and even then, I had an older Punjabi nanny and staff that spent more time with me than my parents did."

"It was you and your brother?"

Ravi nodded. "Before he became a complete douchebag when he went off to college, we just had each other. We would go on these adventures by ourselves. We had some woods near our house, and we would spend hours exploring or pretending we were trying to find buried treasure. We also did this soapbox derby in our town where we used to build these soapbox cars every year. My brother would want to make it go as fast as possible, and I'd create this elaborate story behind it while doing all of the design work. We were such a good team back then that we won four years in a row. It was just what we did, and what all of our friends' parents did, too."

Jessie nodded, even though she hated the picture he'd painted in her mind. Of a sad Ravi sitting alone in a room with all the toys in the world and no one interested enough to play with him. Of his brother, his only friend, leaving him for college, then coming back to be just like his father. It seemed so different from the world she knew, where she was constantly surrounded by members of the community.

There was always a family friend pitching in to raise her, to watch her parents' store when they needed it, to offer a hand. "Sorry. I didn't mean to pry."

"Yes, you did," he said, smiling in earnest now. He adjusted his backward cap. "I know you're not a fan of nepo babies."

She shrugged. "I guess some of them can be nice . . . *sometimes.*"

He laughed, and the sound was like warm sunshine. "If that's your way of saying we should be friends, I'll take it." He motioned to the book in the center of the table. "Were you able to keep your hands off it all weekend?"

Jessie propped her hands on her hips and tilted her chin up. "You know what? I'm not even going to be insulted that you asked me. Because obviously it's very tempting. But no, I didn't open it."

"Nice job. What do we do now, Velma?"

"We get to work, Daphne," she said, the quip rolling off her tongue. Jessie unzipped her backpack and took out a small pen pouch. Then she removed a folder with a few printouts that she'd managed to get from the yearbook office. She'd known to check with the office manager only because one of the other students who worked the information desk with her also volunteered as a photographer for the yearbook club.

Ravi watched her like she was an insect under a microscope, but at least he didn't say anything while she set up.

"We know the name of the person writing the letters because she wrote her name at the bottom of the very first note that we read in Davidson Tower," she said, removing the first piece of paper from the folder. "There was only one Divya Das on campus in 1972." She used a small magnet she usually brought with her and put the paper on the magnetic whiteboard.

"This still doesn't prove that Divya is a part of the legend—"

"No, it doesn't," she said. "We're going to have to try to first figure out who wrote the letters, then determine if there is any connection

95

to the library fire." She looked at the black-and-white picture she was able to pull from the university yearbook archives. In those days, the university had every class take yearbook photos. Jessie had discovered that in late 1990, the policy changed so only graduating class members got their picture in the yearbook.

Thank god for policy changes.

"I could only find one reference of Divya in the yearbook office," Jessie said. "But I cross-checked a bunch of the other South Asian students, and a lot of them only had one picture taken as well."

"Do you think they dropped out?"

"Maybe," Jessie said. "College dropout rates were a lot higher back then. Especially for women."

Divya had only two yearbook photos; her first was from 1971, and the second was 1972. She looked so young, even though she was probably just a year older in the photo than Jessie was now. Her hair was parted in the center and pulled back to a simple knot at the base of her neck. She wore a small red bindi and a simple salwar kameez, judging by the neckline of the bust photo. Did she dress in traditional Indian clothing all the time? Or did she change into pants for classes? Did she ever feel coerced to wear one thing or another? Divya heard the stories from her mother and grandmother. She'd listened to her friends back home. Cliches were truths in the seventies.

"She was beautiful," Ravi said softly.

Jessie turned to her left to see that Ravi had gotten out of his seat and rounded the table to take a closer look at the printout. His jaw was set as he scanned the grainy image.

"Ravi?"

"Mm-hm?"

"How brave do you think she was to have lived a life where she wrote letters and had to hide them in fear of being found out?"

"Brave," Ravi said without thinking. "I have to work myself up to answer the phone now when talking to my father. I can't imagine what hers was like."

Jessie couldn't, either. Divya's parents were immigrants, arriving in a foreign country, with so many beliefs and concepts that didn't apply in their new home. "I'm surprised she was able to go to school."

"Yeah, she must have been loved."

She must have been loved.

Maybe that was the simple answer they weren't taking into account. Love was a powerful motivation. Jessie cleared her throat and took a step back from Ravi. She motioned to the book. "Do you want to do the honors?"

Ravi sat in his chair again. "As a reward for your patience, knock yourself out."

She leaned over and slid the book toward her before lifting the cover again. Each letter was a folded piece of paper with an extended flap that was creased to curl over one edge and seal it as a makeshift envelope. "Do we put these in chronological order first, or read them how they were stacked in the box?"

"I'm sure the order they're currently in means something, but if we're trying to figure out context, it might be a good idea to get the real timeline."

"That's very practical, Ravi Kumar."

He smiled, and it was ever so cocky. "I have my moments."

They worked in tandem, looking at the top of the folded messages for the dates and piling them first by month, then ordering them by day until they were able to create one neat stack. There were fifty-six letters in all, with the first dated September of 1971 and the last dated May of 1972. There were gaps in time that coincided with school breaks and holidays.

"Are you ready to open the first letter?" Ravi asked.

Jessie nodded. She could feel her heart pounding. She picked up the first paper, yellowed at the edges, faded in black ink. Then she ran her finger under the flap, and it opened easily, as if it had been read many times before.

It was all there before her. The handwriting that was indicative of Indian boarding school, because her father had the same kind, and she knew it well. There were subtle flares of personalization, though. Divya drew circles over her *i*'s instead of dots. The tails of her *t*'s were elongated.

"'Dear Jaan—'"

"Jaan," Ravi said. He pressed a hand to his chest. "Do you think he was Indian, too?"

Jessie looked up. She hadn't even gotten into the meat of the letter yet. "Maybe, but isn't the legend that the guy's parents worked for the university?"

"You're still assuming that this is a part of the legend, Jessie," Ravi replied. "What happened to figuring out the letters first?"

"Yeah, you're right. Let's see what else it says."

Jessie read the rest of the letter, and they stopped after each line, discussing any hidden meaning that might be there.

She liked that they were working together. That they were using the study room for a shared purpose. Because in this endeavor, he wasn't a nepo baby and she wasn't uptight. They were just Ravi and Jessie.

After they had finished the first letter, they decided to read two more before they called it quits for the day.

"Hey, Jessie?" Ravi said as she unfolded the next letter in the pile.

"Yeah?"

"Thanks," he said.

"For what?"

"For helping me with my story."

She cocked her head to the side. She had no idea what he was talking about, but he smiled at her. He was happy, and maybe that was enough of an explanation from a friend.

"You're welcome," she said. Then cleared her throat.

"'Dear Jaan, I wish I could focus on my studies today, but thoughts of our conversation from last night keep replaying over and over again in my mind.'"

ELEVEN

Ravi

CHAT GROUP

DEEP: Dude, you haven't been around for a couple weeks. What's going on? Are you still mad about your girlfriend?

RAVI: She's not my girlfriend, but yeah, it was a shitty thing to do.

DEEP: We already said we're sorry. We even apologized. But it's time to come out and play, brother.

VIK: It's not a party without you! If you want, you can bring your girl, and we'll be nice.

RAVI: I'll be out in a week or so, okay? Exams are coming up, and they're kicking my ass. Plus, I'm working on something.

DEEP: Oh yeah? Like an app? I KNEW you had it in you, brother. Can't wait to see you blow up just like the rest of your fam.

KUMAR FAM WHATSAPP GROUP

MUMMA: Ravi, beta, your brother is launching a new app in Boston this weekend. We'd like to see you if possible.

RAVI: I have midterms coming up.

PAPA: That shouldn't stop you from coming out to support your brother. In fact, this is a perfect opportunity to network with some of the executives you'll be working with one day.

RAVI: I think my exams are more important.

ARJUN: Your priorities need to be straightened out, Ravi. Pick an internship and come to the event.

RAVI: You know, the more you act like an asshole, the less likely I am to listen to you, Arjun.

PAPA: Enough, Ravi. You know the right thing to do. Don't disappoint us.

RAVI: I'm sure no matter what I do, I probably will.

iMESSAGE 2:03 p.m.

JESSIE: Hey, I'm waiting in the study room. I found something out about the letters. Hurry up! I'm going to burst if I don't tell someone soon.

Ravi read the text message from Jessie as he walked into the library. He grinned at the slew of happy-face and clapping emojis that expressed her excitement. They hadn't been able to look at the next batch of letters for a couple weeks because they'd both been so busy with work. When Ravi told Jessie that he needed to finish a few papers and get a couple of assignments out of the way, she didn't scoff at him or ask him why he was even bothering like he expected her to. Instead, she gave him the space that he needed, and he was finally able to come up for air.

He cut through the lobby, trying to avoid anyone who was looking in his direction, so they didn't follow him to the basement. As he walked, he thought about his last text exchanges with his friends and his family. They didn't understand why he wanted to graduate with honors. And truthfully, Ravi wasn't sure he'd be able to explain it to them, either.

He took the elevator up to the sixth floor and then waited until the lobby cleared out like he always did before he took the second elevator down to the basement. As usual, there was no one there. The closer he walked to Davidson Tower, the quieter it became until the only noise was from the hum of the air unit.

When he approached the far end of the floor, he saw Jessie through the glass, standing in front of her whiteboard. There was that single picture of Divya Das pinned to an otherwise empty space. Before he stepped into the room, he looked over his shoulder at the Davidson Tower doors. He expected to see the shadows inside and light filtered through the stained-glass windows. Except something was different this time.

He was still staring at Davidson Tower when the study-room door opened.

"Hey," Jessie said. Her hair was in a high ponytail, and she wore a T-shirt and sweatshirt over her jeans. It was her typical outfit that she wore whenever she was studying in the library. "Is something wrong?"

Ravi pointed to Davidson Tower and then walked over with Jessie on his heels. He saw what was different when he was a few feet away.

There was a sign in the window. A small white label that read, "Interested in finding out what plans Hartceller University has for Davidson Tower? Scan the QR code for more details!"

They both took out their cell phones at the same time and held their camera lenses over the small QR code.

"Oh my god," Jessie said as she scrolled on her phone. "They're going to gut the whole thing."

Ravi read the article under the pictures of the tower. "It looks like an anonymous donor, an alumnus with a lot of money, wants to take out all the stained glass. All that beautiful architecture is going to be gone." He looked down at Jessie. "I don't know why they'd want to tear apart what made this place so beautiful."

"It's like a kaleidoscope, and they want to ruin it," she said. Then, as if waking from a daydream, she shook her head. "The best thing we can do is focus on what we can control."

"What's that?"

"The letters," Jessie said. "Do you want to get started on the next set?"

His head was filled with images of kaleidoscopes and mosaics, but he nodded. "Yeah, I'm curious what had you sending me a crap ton of emojis earlier today."

Her eyes lit up, and his thoughts scattered at the sight of her sparkle. She looked so happy, so excited. Had he ever felt that way about something before?

"We missed three letters!" she said. "When we were putting them in chronological order, we missed the first three letters that Divya wrote to her *Jaan*. We didn't start with the first one like we thought."

He felt his heart thump at the thought that there could be more to the story. "Okay, then maybe we should open the first one to find out."

They went back to the study room, and he took his regular position opposite the whiteboard while she sat in front of it. She picked up the weathered piece of paper, one yellowed at the corners with age, more worn than the rest.

"This was stuck to the backside of another letter, which is why we didn't catch it," she said. "But when I was tabbing each stack by date, I felt it and pried it apart. Then I checked the rest of the envelopes and found the other two."

"Okay, but what does it say?" he asked.

Jessie let out a deep breath as if she were preparing herself for bad news. Then she slid her finger between the seams of the folded paper and opened it.

"'Dear Christian.'"

She froze, her head jerking up.

His pulse raced as he got up and rounded the table. He braced his arms on either side of her, crowding her in, smelling the soft floral scent of her hair. The distraction stretched for one heartbeat, then another, before he was able to focus on the words between her trembling fingertips.

"His name is Christian," he said softly, his words fluttering against her ear. "We have a place to start."

"We should probably do some research on how many Christians were enrolled at the time," Jessie said.

He nodded and, with some reluctance, moved away from her and went back to his seat. "I think there are some digital archives we can access through the library database. I'll start there."

They worked in silence for over an hour, combing through records that the school kept in meticulous order. He was sure that they would hit a dead end, but within an hour, he'd amassed more information than he anticipated.

Ravi pushed his computer away from him and crossed his arms over his chest. "I think we finally have a place to start," he said.

"What did you find?"

"Based on digital archives, and the old yearbooks from 1968 through 1972, there are a total of one hundred eighty-seven students during those four years who were named Christian. A couple of them have died, and quite a few of them are on Facebook. But there are maybe seventy that I couldn't find at all. So far, anyway."

Jessie's shoulders slumped. "That's a lot of people with the same name. How are we going to find the one that Divya Das was communicating with?"

"Maybe something in the letters will help us narrow it down. Why don't we start reading the next few letters and see what we can come up with?"

Jessie nodded. "Ravi, I know this is a long shot, but I feel like we might be able to help give closure to this Indian woman's legacy."

There was something about her use of the word *legacy* that made him pause. Was that why it was so important for her to help Divya Das? Because of her legacy? From the brief times they talked about their families and their lives, Ravi knew that Jessie's family didn't have a lot of money. Her goal in school was to become qualified for a job that would pay her a lot so she could help take care of her family the way they'd taken care of her. In a lot of ways, she was alone at Hartceller, too. Was Jessie trying to establish a legacy, or was he reading too much into her tone?

"Come on," he finally said. "Let's read the next few letters."

She grinned, took out the book, and then removed the next letter on top of the pile. Using the tip of one of her pale-pink nails, she opened the flap and unfolded the page. They both read in silence, standing close to each other, hearts beating in rhythm.

Dear Christian, I feel like my life has changed since you entered it. Everything that I see as I walk through the campus grounds reminds me of either conversations that we've had or conversations that I want to have with you. There is a word in Hindi that I thought of when you kissed me for the first time. Jaan. Life. You've been giving me a new life.

"Ugh." Ravi hadn't meant to say it out loud, but the sound escaped through his lips. When Jessie shot him a dirty look, he shrugged. "I'm sorry, but that's sappy as hell."

"Let's just keep reading," she said.

I know my parents want me to have an arranged marriage with the son of one of their childhood friends. Raj is a nice fellow. I've known him since we were children and used to run through the mustard fields behind our homes. It's been some time since I've seen him, but I think he's become an accountant. Like his father. In my family, I would not be able to go out with him prior to the wedding. To eat out in a restaurant and then to see a movie on the green. You held my hand, and I feel as if you are taking my heart.

"Okay, that last line was so bad that I threw up in my mouth," Ravi said.

But Jessie didn't snap at him. She continued to stare at the paper in her hands. Ravi watched as her eyes went back and forth, tracing over each line as if she was committing it to memory.

"It's a first date," she said softly. "I think she's talking about their first date together. Come on, Ravi. You have to believe that they're the couple in the legend, right? It just feels, I don't know, too coincidental not to be them."

His pulse ran a little quicker at the thought. Legends were a funny thing. They felt safe, and amorphous. But once legends became more substantiated, they became frightening. Because what if all those legends could happen to Ravi and Jessie? What if money and status and all the differences that existed in their world outside of school could impact their lives, too?

"Tell me about the first date again," he said, his voice hoarse.

"They went to a restaurant," she said. She cleared her throat and focused on the task at hand. "Then watched a movie together on the green. Is she talking about Thursday-night movies on the green in the center of campus?"

"That's what it sounds like," Ravi said. He'd never been himself, because his friends preferred to drink at the frat house, but he'd heard that a lot of students brought food and drinks and lawn chairs.

"I think that's tonight," Jessie said before she checked her watch. "In a couple of hours."

Ravi reached out and took the paper from her fingertips. It felt brittle in his hand, as if the words delicately laid out on even lines would disappear faster than the smoke from his vape pen. "I just wonder how they were able to see a movie on the green without getting caught. I mean, this is within the first few weeks of them meeting each other. As an interracial couple, they had to be worried that someone would see them and tell their parents. We as South Asians sometimes feel cringy *now* when we're caught by people who may tell someone in our community. In 1971? That had to be a whole different vibe."

Jessie reached across the table and tapped the paper at the very bottom. Her fingertips brushed over his hand, and he felt her touch radiate up his arm. "It says here that there's a place in the science building across from where they set up the projector that had a small balcony where they could stand. I wonder if that's still accessible for students."

"Why, are you interested in taking a date there?" he asked before he could help himself.

He watched her nose wrinkle. "No, but I'm curious to see where it is, to feel closer to Divya while we're reading her letters. I've never been on a date, so I don't think I'll be taking anyone anywhere anytime soon."

His jaw dropped. This beautiful, quirky, infuriating person had never been on a date in her life? Well, the more he thought about it, he guessed that was possible. But not due to lack of opportunity. He was sure it was because Jessie was stubborn. She probably had tunnel vision all through high school, too.

Ravi knew it was a bad idea, but he wanted to be her first. "Go out with me," he said.

"*What?*"

"Go out with me. Let's go to the same restaurant, and let's go see the movie on the green. We can try to find the balcony that Divya used for her first date. I want to take you out."

Her shock turned into understanding. "That's a great idea."

"Wait, it is?"

She nodded, her ponytail bobbing. "Yeah, definitely. We can both just retrace the steps of the entire date. Maybe it'll give us some insight into their lives."

Just as he thought, Ravi mused. She was stubborn.

"And we can take a break and go out. Together."

There was that confusion again, but he didn't bother giving her any additional explanation. She'd probably talk herself out of it.

"Okay," Jessie finally said. "It's a . . . well, it's a date."

"Great," he said, and leaned back in his chair. "Let's finish here, and then maybe we can pack up our things and head straight to dinner. Where did the letter say that they went out to eat?"

"Rothby's. Oh! That's the place we went the first night we found the book. The one with the excellent truffle fries."

Ravi grinned at her excitement. She looked her age when she brightened with happiness. Young and eager to try every new experience college had to offer. Did he ever look as excited and happy as she did right in this moment? Maybe that's why he was so drawn to spend time with her. Because these moments were fleeting. They were special, and he wanted to be a part of them with her. Better yet, he wanted to be the one to give them to her. "I guess we're going to Rothby's," he said, then watched, grinning, as she cheered.

TWELVE

Jessie

Jessie could not believe a person who looked as sweet and as delicate as Divya would frequent a place like Rothby's. Maybe it looked different in 1971, but in the present day and age, it was a typical diner with worn leather seats, scratched melamine plates, the stale stench of coffee, and a rotating dessert rack that displayed cakes and pies bigger than a human head. She had noticed all the details the first time she'd visited with Ravi, but the second time around, knowing that the place was familiar to Divya, it seemed even more charming.

"Do you think she wore a poodle skirt here?" Ravi asked as they slid into one of the booths in the back of the diner.

"Wrong decade," Jessie replied.

Outside the windows, groups of students walked to the nearest bars and restaurants or up to Greek Hill. It was a welcome distraction from the fact that they were both sitting together, having dinner, and then going to a movie like a real date. Except she wasn't sure if this was a real date.

The corner of his lips curved in the way she'd come to like. "Can I tell you something, Jessie Jaissi Koi Nahin?"

There was a flutter in her belly at the nickname. "Is it the reason why you call me that ridiculous nickname?"

He paused. "I call you the nickname because I've never met anyone else like you, and you do such a great job at hiding how beautiful you are, but I'm lucky enough to see it."

She faltered. "Really?"

This time he looked confused. "What did you think I meant? You're obviously not ugly, if that's what you thought."

The explanation warmed her heart, and she had to work hard at hiding the tremble in her fingers. When did he become such a romantic?

Before the thought finished forming in her head, she knew the answer. He was always a romantic to her. From the very first night he walked her home. "I'll accept that explanation," she said. "If what you want to tell me isn't about my nickname, then what is it?"

He combed his fingers through his hair before he put on his hat backward. "I'm writing this story. It's just for me, something ridiculous that I'm sure will never see the light of day. And I imagine the place where my protagonist spends most of his time is a diner just like this."

"Oh yeah? How far into writing it are you?"

"Maybe a hundred pages."

Jessie watched the excitement play on his face. He loved this project he was working on, and it made him happy. The same way she imagined his parents wanted him to feel with the future they'd designed for him.

"That's amazing! I can't imagine writing a hundred pages of fiction. That's some serious talent. Will you tell me about it? The story, I mean."

"Yeah, I guess," he said. "When it's done, you can read it if you want."

The fluttering grew stronger, because when he beamed at her, she realized that he must not have told many people about his project. "If you're writing stories, I guess that means you don't want to be a big tech genius like your father and brother?"

The smile slipped off his face, and she was sorry to see it go. "I don't think I can," he said. "They're the type of innovators that come around once in a century. Who wants to compete with that? I'm not special like them."

You are.

Jessie cleared her throat and picked up one of the plastic menus, turning to the first page. "If you aren't going to become the next big software engineer, what are you going to do after you graduate?"

The lines around Ravi's mouth deepened. "I don't know."

"Well, if I had your legacy, I know that I would use it to my advantage to get noticed by every internship and job I possibly could."

The corner of his lip quirked. "You would?"

She nodded. "Can I tell you a secret?"

He leaned forward. "Tell me."

She could feel her cheeks get hot at how close he was. "I'm terrible at interviews. I just start rambling, and then I get super nervous. I mean, I overprepare to the point where it should be a no-brainer that I should get the job or internship, but my nerves get the best of me. I don't think I've ever gotten the exact internship I've wanted because somehow I've always screwed it up."

He let out a whistle. "That's a secret I wasn't expecting to hear."

"It's true," she said. "I mean, there was this one time where I was in this interview, and the hiring manager had an elephant statue on their shelf behind their desk. It was one of those things that people buy to take up space. A bargain-shelf buy from Target. Anyway, the hiring manager asked me how my trip was to the office, and all I could talk about was the fact that in certain villages in India, elephants destroyed entire crop fields. That's when a scientist found out that elephants are afraid of bees and started putting speakers that emit bee sounds along a sanctuary perimeter, and now they're called bee fences. He just stared at me after that."

"'Bee fences'? Wait, are you serious?"

"You don't have to laugh—"

"I'm not," he said. "I can't imagine that's easy to admit. I mean, you're always so . . . perfect."

"I'm only telling you my secrets because I trust you."

"You do?"

The sparkle in his eyes was enough to make her realize that she'd probably shared more than she should've. She cleared her throat and shifted in her seat so that she could get some space between them. "Now if someone like you was nervous, I doubt it would matter. Like we've already established, you have a name. And there are enough people in your family who've found success in the tech field. There has to be some sort of Kumar training manual, right?"

Ravi scoffed. "Yeah, it's called listening to my parents and doing what I'm told."

"Oh, you don't like that," she said, scanning the menu.

Ravi curled two fingers over the top of her menu and pulled it down to the table so they could see each other. "What do you mean?"

The lines around his mouth deepened. Paired with the shadows in his eyes, he looked distracted and so, so tired. Jessie put down the menu.

"I mean, you're determined to figure out what you want to do with your life on your own, no matter how messy and complicated your path might be. We may not know each other well, but in the time since we've met, you get up at 7:00 a.m. to block out specific days in our studying room. You've walked me home every night, and you point out the flaws in all of my arguments because you still don't believe in happily ever after. That tells me you're just as stubborn as I am."

He was smiling again. The lines were gone. "I think it's hard to be as stubborn as you, Jessie Jaissi Koi Nahin."

Their waitress, a woman older than Father Time, stepped up to their table. She had a helmet of white hair that reminded Jessie of one of the Golden Girls and wore a faded yellow uniform with a white collar and white apron. "Can I get you kids anything to drink first?"

Jessie looked over at Ravi, who gave an imperceptible shake of his head. She ignored his warning, then glanced down at her name tag.

"Hi, Ms. Sylvia. Yes, I think we're ready with our drinks, but I have a question for you first, if you don't mind?"

"Sure, honey," Sylvia said, cocking her hip to the side.

"How long have you been working at Rothby's?"

She let out a low whistle. "Since the sixties at least. I was sixteen when I got my job here. Thirty-five when I bought the place."

"You own the diner?" Ravi asked.

Jessie almost expected him to sound condescending, but there was only excitement and interest in his voice. A small part of her seemed to relax at the realization that he wasn't going to judge Sylvia.

Sylvia nodded. "I do own the place! Love it. I pitch in when I need a bit of exercise. Went to the university. Are you students?"

"Yes, ma'am," Ravi said. "We're actually taking this class together on nonfiction writing, and I think we want to write about the library fire in the seventies."

Jessie didn't know if she was imagining things, but something seemed to flicker across Sylvia's face. Maybe it was just an awareness or acknowledgment that the story had become legend. Or maybe, Jessie thought, it was something more.

"I'm sorry, kids, I don't know if I can help you there. That was a long time ago."

"We think that there was an Indian woman who was involved," Jessie added. "There were so few back then. Nothing like how it is today. She probably came here."

This time Sylvia smiled. "And what makes you think that?"

"Besides the excellent truffle fries? It's the best place to bring a date if you're trying to be secretive about it. All you would have to do is take your textbooks out and put them to the side. Then people would think that you're just studying. It's close enough to campus that it's completely plausible."

Sylvia nodded. "I guess you're right." She looked back at the counter, at the booths filled with couples and crowds. "I'll tell you this, and you can quote me as Sylvia Robertson in your papers. After the fire, there was a group of official-type folks who came into the diner, showing pictures of a bunch of different kids who were missing from their dorm rooms that night. I recognized them. One or two of them were Indian for sure. But those official types never came back. I assumed that everyone was accounted for after that, ya know?"

Jessie sighed. It was clear Sylvia didn't remember Divya, and it was even less likely she'd know the man she had dined with all those decades ago.

Jessie looked at Ravi, who shook his head. He didn't want her to press anymore, either.

"Ms. Sylvia? I'll have tea if you have it. Black, preferably. And definitely a plate of those truffle fries."

"I'll have the coffee, thank you," Ravi said.

Ms. Sylvia left, and Ravi leaned over the table so that they were close enough for their breath to mingle and she could see the rich, dark brown of his eyes.

"That wasn't very subtle."

"I think with a story that's over fifty years old, subtlety is overrated."

Ravi looked like he was thinking about it for a moment before he said, "I guess it was effective. Now can we try to enjoy our date?"

Her arms tingled as a stretch of goose bumps formed. "I thought the whole purpose of this was to re-create the date that Divya and Christian had when they came to Rothby's and went to the movies."

"It's also because you've never been on a date before," Ravi replied. He crossed his arms and leaned on the table. "And now you're on a date."

"Ravi," she said, knowing that her laughter sounded fraught with nerves. She was just going to be straightforward, so they both could keep their expectations low. "You don't have to take pity on me. You're a third-year and someone who will probably have a great relationship with a woman who makes just as much money as you will. I'll eventually date. We'll just call this what it is. Research."

She looked over his shoulder and saw that there was a group of Desi kids glancing their way. They served as her reminder that this moment in time with Ravi was a fever dream. It would be something that she could tell her family in twenty years when his name would appear on the board of directors of some tech conglomerate. And after she'd shared the memory, she'd think of this moment where he wore his backward hat, a gray sweatshirt with the university logo on the front, and slight scruff on his jaw. That visual would be just for her.

"First of all, this isn't pity," Ravi said. "I'm considering this a real date. I'm taking a pretty woman out for dinner and a movie."

If she could blush, she would. "I don't think this is about how much of a snack I am—"

"And second of all, what's so bad about dating? Are you planning on just holding off until you get that career you want? What about all the experiences you'll miss along the way?"

Jessie tried to relax, tried to pretend that the compliment didn't affect her the way it had. "Sometimes you have to make sacrifices in order to get what you want in the long run. I have my books and my labs and my work-study job at the information desk. I need all of that to get the best job I can possibly get. I have to be better than most in this economy, and because I don't have connections."

She didn't mean to poke at his family name again and hated herself for the way he winced at the word *connections*.

"I understand sacrifices," he started, "but what if you don't have to make them? What if you're just telling yourself you have to make them because it's easier that way instead of opening yourself up?"

Her heart started to pound. He was close, too close to the truth. A truth she wasn't even sure she was willing to admit to herself, let alone vocalize. Because if she was honest with herself, she'd have to confront the fact that she had been avoiding emotional entanglements, choosing to focus solely on her schoolwork. It was a protective barrier she had built around her heart to shield herself from potential pain. As a teenager, she'd been captivated by romance novels and movies. It was thrilling to be swept away by these fantasies, but she couldn't ignore the undercurrent of caution that ran through each story—the inevitable heartbreak. "I can choose not to date if I want to."

Ravi shrugged. "Yeah, absolutely. But you still chose to go out with me."

"Here we are," Sylvia called out as she brought their drinks to the table. "Did you two have some time to think about what you want to eat? Other than the fries, of course."

Jessie looked down at her closed menu. "I'm so sorry, Ms. Sylvia. We were chatting. Do you think you can give us a minute so we can figure it out? We promise we'll be quick."

Ms. Sylvia waved a dismissive hand. "Take your time, dear. You two are so adorable. I'll tell you what, after years of experience: the dates where you just can't tell time and you're just gabbing away are the good ones. Hold on to each other."

After she left, Ravi gave her a smug look.

"What?"

He reached out and took her hand. The touch of his fingertips against hers had her jolting in her seat. The soft skin of his palm, the rough pads of his fingertips. She held her breath as he looked at her in the eyes.

"Ravi?"

"What's so bad about going out with someone like me?" he asked.

Her ears were ringing now. She slowly pulled her hand away from Ravi's grasp. "Because we're living in a pressure chamber. One that has kaleidoscope colors and makes us believe that anything is possible. College is not the real world. It's a fantasy."

He scoffed. "I know fantasy, Jessie, and this is more real than anything I've ever experienced."

She shook her head, and her heart pounded like a drum. Ravi wanted this to be real. He wanted their date to mean something. Why couldn't he see how different they both were? "Look, after you leave in a year, you're going to be as legendary as Divya Das. Students will be talking about you for decades and how you once walked these halls before you became a big shot in the tech industry. Literally. And me? I'll be an engineer. A corporate drone who works hard and tries to chase a promotion every few years."

"I don't think that you would ever—"

"I can't risk falling for you," she snapped. The truth tumbled out, more dramatic than she'd ever intended, but she didn't know how else to get through to him. How else to stop the . . . attachment she was beginning to feel toward him. The jealousy she had whenever he smiled at someone else, and the softness in her heart when she went to sleep thinking about how she was safe because she knew Ravi would make sure of it. "My roots are too shallow, and one strong storm in my life, my entire future will topple to the ground."

The deep grooves along his mouth were back. "We can build those roots while we're in school. Let's—"

"No," she said softly. She shook her head, causing her hair to slide over her shoulder. "Let's focus on Divya Das. Once we find closure for her, we'll find our closure, too."

He looked like he wanted to ask her more. A part of her wished that he would so she could just put it all out in the open—the tension that existed between them and the fact that they belonged to two completely separate universes.

But all Ravi did was lean back in his seat and cross his arms over his chest. "Okay," he said.

"Okay?" she asked.

"Okay," he repeated. "Hey, do you eat meat? The bacon cheeseburger is good."

OCTOBER 1, 1971

Dear Christian,

Please don't be upset with me. If we were seen, then the safe haven we've created in the kaleidoscope room may be destroyed. I would love to share a meal with you, to be courted like my American friends. But I don't see a future for us if that were to happen.

THIRTEEN

Ravi

avi was pretty sure he'd never been rejected before. He didn't
know if that was an absurdly cocky thing to think or if he was
just being honest with himself. It's just that he'd never had a
chance to shoot his shot and be put down so quickly and efficiently.

After dinner, they headed to the movie out on the green. Just like
the letter had said, they found the hidden balcony where they could
see the projector. They were able to sneak out chairs from the adjacent
classroom without setting off any alarms, so they didn't have to sit on
the cold floor, which was nice.

While they watched, Ravi remembered the cult classic movie
Twilight. Edward and Bella in the chemistry lab. Edward couldn't stand
the smell of Bella because he wanted her so much. And damn if Ravi
didn't understand for the first time how smell was intoxicating.

Not that he wanted to suck Jessie's blood or anything, but he was
hyperaware of the woman sitting next to him, and it was a whole new
experience for him.

Then, like every night after they studied in the library, he walked
her back to her dorm, winked, and then headed to his condo.

He hadn't written in a few days, but the next morning, he sat at
his desk with a cup of coffee and his half-finished document. Deep in
his consciousness, he knew that Jessie was the reason he felt inspired.

Because of their time together, he was compelled to create. And because she was his muse, he wanted her advice and input even though she would likely encourage him to trust his instincts. Because that was exactly the type of advice that Jessie would give him.

While Ravi sipped his coffee, he added a few paragraphs to what was shaping up to be a narrative that felt more personal than he'd planned, and then sat back to look at his work. When the words didn't come anymore, he packed his bag and headed to the library to meet with the person who dominated his thoughts.

As he crossed the courtyard, Ravi waved to some familiar faces who called his name, before entering the rear entrance of the library. He completed his regular elevator routine but was disappointed when he got to their study room on the basement level and found it empty.

His pulse quickened at the thought that something might have happened to Jessie.

RAVI: Hey, I'm in the study room. Where are you?

JESSIE: Hey, I'm so sorry I forgot to tell you. My parents ended up surprising me this morning. They both flew in for parents' weekend. I'm out today through Sunday.

Parents' weekend. Ravi remembered when his parents showed up during his first year. The president and the deans of the STEM departments wanted meeting after meeting. Since that experience, he'd asked his folks not to show up. He always gave one excuse or another as to why they shouldn't come.

RAVI: No sweat. Have fun.

JESSIE: Thanks.

Maybe this was a good time to hang out with the guys he hadn't seen for a while. Since he'd become so busy with Jessie, his brothers had grown increasingly demanding of his time. Some of their folks probably weren't in town yet, at least not until Saturday afternoon. That meant he had all of Friday night.

He left the library and was walking toward the shuttle stop that he planned on taking to his building when his phone buzzed. Jessie's name appeared on the screen. He didn't even have to think twice about answering when he usually avoided calls.

"Hello?"

"Hey," she said, her voice slow and cautious. "Please say no."

"No to what?"

There was the sound of hushed whispering and quick exchanges in the background. Jessie sighed. "My parents saw that I was texting *a friend* and they would love to meet you. They want to extend an invitation for brunch tomorrow morning at 10:00 a.m. Only if you're interested. There's a Pancake House about ten minutes' walk from the freshman dorm that's close to their hotel. Join us if you'd like."

Ravi grinned. "You know what, Jessie? I think I will."

"Ravi, please have mercy—" she whispered.

"I'll see you tomorrow," he said cheerfully, and hung up. He grinned at his phone, a sense of excitement for the first time in a while coursing through his bloodstream.

His weekend got infinitely better.

Ravi had never met the parents of a girl he was dating. He'd met Sahdna's parents plenty of times at fundraisers and different events back in San Fran, before they had gone out a few times and decided they were better off as friends. But he didn't know them because he was dating their daughter. They just happened to go to the same parties. This brunch with Jessie's parents was different.

The night before, he did a ton of research, scrolling through all her social media, studying the pictures she posted with her parents and her brother. He went to the university store first thing in the morning.

When he got to the Pancake House, Jessie was standing outside on the sidewalk with two older Indian parents. Jessie's mom wore capris and a visor, while her dad wore a polo shirt tucked into the jeans he had hiked up to his midtorso.

"Hello, Ahuja family!" he said once he was within hearing distance.

"Oh my god," Jessie said, covering her face with one hand.

"You must be my daughter's friend," Jessie's mother said. She approached him with her arms held wide. Ravi put the bag on the ground and returned her hug.

She smelled like spice and flowers, different from his own mother, who always smelled like expensive French perfume.

"It's great to meet Jessie's parents," he said. He held out a hand to Jessie's father. "Sir."

"Oh please. Call me Uncle."

"Okay, Uncle. It's nice to meet you."

"You as well! Were you doing some shopping this morning?" Jessie's father pointed to the bulging bag that he'd left on the sidewalk.

"Oh, this is for you," Ravi said, and picked up the bag to give it to Jessie's father. "The student center was giving out free sweatshirts and T-shirts and hats to the first one hundred people there that morning. I just happened to be walking through and getting my cup of coffee and realized that you might want some official Hartceller University gear."

Jessie crossed her arms over her chest. Her expression was mutinous. "I literally worked the information desk this morning, Ravi. There were no plans for giveaways."

"I think it was a last-minute decision by the student body." Ravi motioned to the bag. "They had some great stuff for parents' weekend."

Jessie's father took out the sweatshirt that read, "HARTCELLER DAD." There was a matching hat, mug, and T-shirt. The smile on his face was worth the deception. Underneath it were matching sweatshirts in red and white, the university's colors, for Jessie's mother.

"We were planning to go to the university bookstore after brunch," Jessie's mother said as she slipped the sweatshirt over her head and refastened her visor. "We were hoping that there was some sort of sale this weekend so we could get a magnet. This is so much more than we imagined! You've picked out the perfect items in just the right size."

"You're welcome. My parents have a few things from their first parents' weekend, too."

Their eyes widened. Jessie's father reached out and clapped Ravi on the shoulder. "Your father has made a name for the Indian community. We're proud of him."

"I am, too," Ravi said. *Even if he's never proud of me.*

An employee wearing all black pushed open the front door and shouted to the sparse crowd outside. "Ahuja, party of four!"

Jessie's mother raised her hand. "That's us! Come on, our table is ready."

Jessie held Ravi's arm until her parents went ahead of them. She leaned in close and whispered, "What in the world are you doing?"

Ravi shrugged. "I have no idea what you're talking about."

"There was no giveaway at the student center, was there?"

"I told you," Ravi said innocently. "Last-minute kinda thing."

He tried to follow her parents, but Jessie gripped his arm to hold him back. "Hey," she said. "Thanks. You didn't have to do that for my folks, but I appreciate it. They never would have been able to afford all that stuff. You made their day."

Ravi looked around to see if anyone was watching. Then he lifted a hand and ran his thumb over the curve of her jaw. She stiffened, but she didn't pull away.

"Thanks for inviting me," he said. He registered her shock, the slight confusion and insecurity that flashed in her expression. Then he walked to the restaurant entrance to open the door for Jessie.

Ravi expected to be fielding questions for the entire brunch about his family, about AI or the future of technology, and about any of the salacious drama in Silicon Valley. Instead, he was pleasantly surprised to find that Jessie's parents were more interested in him. They asked what his major was, what classes he liked, what he did on the weekends, and if he had any favorite movies or books.

He felt humanized. He felt like he was his own person.

Jessie squirmed in her seat the entire time, but he could see that despite her discomfort, she was really happy to see her parents. She welcomed their casual touches, her mother's frequent hugs.

"Ravi," Jessie's mom started when the food had arrived. "What are your plans for after college? Are you going back to the West Coast?"

He felt his throat tighten, then glanced at Jessie, who focused on the plate in front of her. "I think so. The other option is grad school."

"That's very good," Jessie's father said. "I have my master's, and it served me well over the years."

"Does it help you with your business?"

He rested his forearms against the edge of the table as he forked a tiny triangle of pancakes. "It helped me when I was an engineer."

Ravi barely controlled his jaw from dropping. "You were an engineer?"

Jessie's father's shoulders straightened, and he smiled proudly. "I was. IBM had sponsored my visa. Jessie's mother and I were both international employees. Then I was laid off. I was lucky enough to get another job quickly that continued to sponsor my visa, but I knew I had to start thinking about what would happen if I was laid off again. We saved all of our money, we were able to apply for the green card, and then after I qualified, I left my job and put all of my savings into the store that I've been running ever since. That store has helped us thrive as a family even though we don't have much."

Jessie laid a hand on her father's arm, her smile warm and genuine. "You and Mama have always been the best, Papa."

"No, you're the best, my beta," he said, and patted her hand.

They shared a look filled with so much love that Ravi felt home-sick for the first time he could remember. Maybe he should go visit his father and talk about this internship in person. He could even mention his manuscript, but he doubted that would be met with warmth and understanding.

No, he thought. Talking to his father was never worth his time. There had never been a single moment where he felt understood by him.

"You're all really lucky to have each other," he said.

Jessie's parents smiled at him, their faces beaming with joy. It was the same happiness that Jessie would share with him in fleeting moments. Now he knew where she got it from.

And he felt so ashamed that it burned in his gut like churning bile. Sure, Jessie was serious, but why wouldn't she be the kind of person who grew up happy? Just because her life had been different from his didn't mean it was less than or worse off than his had been. If anything, it was better. She had people who appreciated and loved her for who she was, and as cheesy as it sounded, that was something that money couldn't buy.

"Now, Jessie," her mother said. "Why don't you tell us what you two have been up to? Are you dating?"

"Oh my god, Mom, no, I told you we're working on a project together for class."

"Oh? What project is that?"

Jessie looked at him, and for the first time that day, her smile was for him. "It's actually a really interesting story. It involves a woman who wrote a bunch of letters. There's a chance she is part of a campus legend that people talk about to this day. But you can't tell anyone."

FOURTEEN

Jessie

Jessie felt like they were missing something. They had been in the study room for the last couple of hours trying to find out everything they could about the missing-person reports that were filed in 1972. She had hoped the letters would be a little bit more transparent about the things they did or where they were or the people they knew. But instead, there were only tiny clues that required internet searches and lots of archive reading.

Ravi propped his feet on the table and pulled his hood over his head. "Don't you think we're trying a little too hard to figure out what they were doing instead of where they went?"

"We don't want to miss important details," Jessie said. "This is how we understand them, right?"

"I guess so. But, Jessie, what if all of this is just a stack of letters and it doesn't tell us much more than the fact that two people fell in love?"

Jessie felt a pang in her chest. "Then I would be really sad that I couldn't find out what happened to Divya."

Ravi dropped his feet to the floor and then rounded the table. The closer he came, the harder it was for her to control her fidgeting. She worried the dry erase marker between her fingers, moving it back and forth.

"You have to remember," he said quietly as he leaned against the table facing the whiteboard with her. "If you make this about anything more than uncovering a story, you may just be disappointed, right? We've found her name. We can use that for our paper."

Jessie looked down at the open book, and the stack of neatly folded letters that they had put to the side after reading and dissecting. There weren't that many to go, and she couldn't help but feel like she was losing a little faith. Maybe these were only the letters that Christian left behind? He might have taken the ones that meant the most to him since he was missing, too.

Jessie's arm bumped against Ravi's as she looked at the mess of notes on the whiteboard.

"I understand if you don't want to do this anymore," she said quietly.

"I'm no quitter," he said. He nudged her with his elbow. "Come on, maybe we should stop for the day and switch to doing some homework."

"I guess you're right," Jessie said. "I have a big physics exam next week, and I feel like even though I'm prepped for it, I need to keep my head in the game."

There was that crooked smile again. "I don't think you have to sweat your exams too much. I bet your parents would be proud of whatever you got."

"I know, but I need to keep my scholarship."

"Hey," Ravi said. She turned around to look at him. "I know I already said it, but I'm going to say it again. Thanks for inviting me to brunch last weekend. Your parents are great."

"They are," Jessie said. "They worked really hard to give me a great life." Jessie picked up her phone and took a picture of the whiteboard. She thought about his parents and remembered that Ravi said he never felt supported by them. That he was the stereotype for filthy-rich kids. Raised by staff and shown affection only by people who were paid to do it. She turned to look at him.

"Can I ask you a question? Do your parents care about your grades? I mean, it's no secret that they expect you to join the family company after you graduate."

Ravi was shaking his head before she finished. "I think as long as I graduate, they don't care. But getting good grades matters to me. Just don't tell people I said that. I'd like to keep some things secret."

Jessie made a motion of zipping her mouth shut and throwing away the key. Then she picked up the board eraser. "But you do get good grades."

He shrugged.

"Ravi . . ."

He held up his hands. "I get good grades because it's something I can control. They're a reflection of my own efforts. The TAs who review my tests don't care about my parents. Most of them don't even know who they are. So yeah, I get good grades because that's something that I can do for myself."

If she hadn't come to like him since their first encounter, she would have liked him now. Jessie respected his determination. It was something that she tried so hard to cultivate in her soul, so she recognized it in someone else.

"Okay," she said as she turned to wipe down their notes on the board.

She was about to erase the column about Divya's lover, Christian, when Ravi placed a hand on her wrist.

"What is it?" she asked. He was close enough that she could smell the rich, clean scent of his cologne.

"You know the information we pulled from the yearbook archives? Do we have a list of last names from the Christians who were around at that time?" Ravi asked.

Jessie sat down and turned her laptop so that Ravi could see the screen, then pulled up an Excel spreadsheet where she had been logging details. "I'm sure it's here somewhere."

They began to scan the spreadsheet, heads tilted close together, knees touching. Jessie's heart began to pound as they scrolled to the end of the data. Was there something here that they missed?

"What are you looking for?"

Ravi tapped the screen, pointing to the column next to the names. "I was thinking about grades and then remembered the part of the story that one of the lovers was related to someone who worked for the university. I wonder if any of the last names here would show up in the emeritus database?"

"I guess we could try," Jessie said. "But there is a chance that there is no correlation, either. Parts of the legend may just have been made up because it sounds better when people are trying to scare each other, telling stories at parties."

Before Ravi could reply, his phone began to buzz on the opposite side of the table. He made a grab for it and looked at the screen. "That's strange. She usually doesn't call . . ."

Jessie started to stand. "Do you want me to—"

Ravi rested a hand on her shoulder and pushed her back down in her seat. He answered.

"Hi, Sahdna, what's up?"

There was a sound of muffled conversation from the other end, most of it in Hindi. She could pick up a couple of words, but Sahdna spoke way too fast. Then Ravi's body went tense, and his hands fisted until his knuckles whitened.

"*What?*" Ravi said. "How did they find out?"

There was another pause, more muffled conversation; then Ravi began to swear. "I don't want them to know where I am. They'll be down here every day if they find us."

Another pause. Jessie could see the clenching of his jaw from across the table.

"Yeah, we'll go. Thanks. And tell Tanvi I said thank you, too."

The mention of her roommate made Jessie wary, and she whipped around to look at him. "What?"

He said a quick goodbye before he hung up the phone. "Sahdna is with Tanvi," he replied.

"That's . . . okay. I mean, other than the fact that Tanvi didn't *tell* me that she's hanging out with Sahdna, what does that have to do with you?" Her anxiety surged, like a car jack lifting the rear end of a sedan.

He ran his fingers through his hair, accidentally knocking off his hat, which fell to the floor. "She was giving me a heads-up," he said, putting his hat firmly back on his head. He tugged the visor low to shadow his face. "Vik and Deep called her, asking if she knew where I was. They're on their way to the library, looking for me for some bro intervention or something. She mentioned it to Tanvi, who was with her at the time. Tanvi said that we're both here together, and we may want to leave before they show up."

"Okay," Jessie said. She started packing her things into her backpack. If his friends were coming to the library, she didn't want to be there, either, in case they found her and interrogated her about Ravi's whereabouts. Especially when they knew they shared a study room. "I'm going to get out of here, too."

He pulled up his hood and slung his designer backpack over his shoulder. His eyes briefly flickered down toward her bag from high school, a ratty gray Jansport that struggled to contain all her textbooks. "Actually," he said. "I have a favor to ask. Come with me back to my condo."

"*What?*"

"Come with me," he said again. "I think we're onto something with Christian's last name, and I don't want to wait to read the next letter. I feel safe in my condo, and I know we won't be disturbed by my friends."

"Why don't we just wait until your friends go away?"

"Who knows when that'll be?" He checked his wristwatch again. "Come on. Knowing Deep and Vik, we don't have much time."

He opened the study-room door, and after another moment of hesitation, Jessie looped her backpack over her shoulder and made the decision to follow Ravi home for the first time since they met. "Fine, let's go."

Without another word, Ravi led her through the basement, up through the lobby, and out the building's side entrance. They walked in silence, like they often did when they were heading to her dorms late at night. But this time, they were heading through the small city center toward the high-rises that were flanked with restaurants, bars, and shops.

"I feel like I'm in a John Wick movie," she whispered.

He stopped in his tracks and turned to look down at her. "A John Wick movie," he said, deadpan. "Seriously?"

She shrugged. "Yeah?"

He shook his head, then continued to lead her across campus. When they reached the outer perimeter of buildings, she nudged his arm.

"I thought you lived on campus close to your fraternity brothers."

"I like my privacy," he said. He then crossed the street, his knuckles brushing hers as they moved close together on the sidewalk before making a left onto a pathway that ended in front of a doorman building encased in glass and steel.

With her nerves rising like a tide, she followed him past the doorman through a marble-and-glass lobby to a set of elevators that required a key card. In the small confines of the polished silver elevator, Jessie let out a deep breath, feeling the air thin in the confines of the space she shared with Ravi.

He still didn't look at her, didn't speak as they ascended.

When they reached his floor, he led her halfway down the hallway, where he used a fingerprint scanner to open his front door.

"Welcome to my home," he said, a slight tremble in his voice.

He stepped aside to let her enter, and she wanted to ask if he was nervous having her over, to tease him about the number of women he'd probably invited home.

"Whoa," she said as she looked around.

To the left of the front door, a small kitchen flowed into an inviting living space that had a couch, coffee table, and two armchairs, all aligned toward a flat-screen TV with speakers on either side. The room's far wall was made of glass and had a beautiful view of the downtown and campus area. Everything was absolutely spotless. The counters were wiped clean, and the coffee table had a small leather-lined tray with one remote and a neat stack of coasters. There were no tapestries, no band posters or school-spirit banners purchased from the bookstore. No, this condo belonged to an adult. The kind that had lived on their own for quite a while.

Jessie tried to make sense of everything she knew so far about Ravi Kumar.

He studied for his tests. He kept his condo spotless. He checked out the same study room she loved at the same times six days a week. He bought gifts for her parents and pretended he didn't so her parents would accept them. And he took her out on her first date, which was one of the best nights that she'd ever had.

Ravi toed off his sneakers to reveal white socks that didn't have any holes in them. Then he dropped his backpack into a chair. "Want to set up here or in the living room? I can order some pizza from that new place I was telling you about."

Jessie knew that her spiraling was getting out of control. "Ah, if I'm getting pizza, I want—"

"Ham, pineapple, and jalapeños. I know."

"How in the world do you know that?" she blurted out.

"You mentioned it on our date last week," Ravi said. He opened the fridge and pulled out two cans of seltzer water. He tossed one to Jessie, and she caught it easily.

"Let me get this straight," she said as she stepped into the kitchen. She put the can down on the counter. "You remembered my pizza order that I said in passing last week? And you want to buy pizza for us while we read letters?"

He gave her a wary look. "It's the least I can do, considering my friends may find our study room."

"So it's a gratitude thing. Just like your reading letters to make up for the fact that your friends locked me in Davidson Tower."

"What? No. Well, yes. Partly," he said, his voice stuttering as she grew closer, taking up his space. "Jessie, what are you doing?"

"I'm asking the questions," she said. "I have another one. When was the last time you vaped?"

He clenched his jaw. "Why do you ask?"

"Because the answer is important to me," she said. She was standing in front of him now, inches away. "When did you last vape, Ravi?"

Ravi leaned back against the fridge. "I don't know. Two weeks ago, maybe?"

Jessie grinned. "You did it for me."

"Shit, Jessie, of course I did it for you. I like you—"

He wasn't able to finish his sentence, because Jessie reached up to cup his face between her palms. Looking into his eyes, she drew him closer so she could press her lips against his. For a moment, he stood frozen, then his arms wrapped around her waist, pulling her close. His mouth glided over hers, and she closed her eyes, drowning in the feel of him.

Then she couldn't think at all. Because Ravi Kumar wasn't just her first date; he was also her first kiss, and the experience was nothing short of magical.

OCTOBER 21, 1971

Dear Jaan,

Your kiss has given me life. The feel of your mouth against mine is a memory I'll keep in my heart forever.

FIFTEEN

Ravi

"S he kissed me; then she ran away like she was being chased by a mob of demons," Ravi said. "I don't even know what I'm supposed to do now." It had been a week, but he felt like it had happened seconds ago. The soft, firm pressure of her fingertips as they curled around the back of his neck and into his hair. The smooth pillow feel of her mouth against his. The curve of her hips as he pulled her close and into his embrace. His pulse was racing in overdrive, and he felt drunk with the sensation of her. That's why he wasn't able to react fast enough to ask her to stay before she slipped out the door without another word.

"I don't know how to tell you this," Sahdna said as she dabbed at the lipstick she'd just reapplied for her social-media feed, "but she may be a lost cause. Jessie has her entire college career in front of her, and she's probably just testing her boundaries."

"Testing her *boundaries?*"

Sahdna shrugged. "Yeah, you know. Kissing guys who are for right now, not forever. That's what Tanvi thinks."

Ravi took a sip of the lukewarm beer. He never understood why they always had to drink the cheap shit at the parties. It's not like they couldn't afford something better. "Jessie isn't the kind of person to kiss someone just because she's testing boundaries. No, if she kisses someone, it means something."

Sahdna raised a perfectly arched brow. "And you know this how?"

"I just do, okay?"

She held up her free hand in surrender. "Hey, you came to me for advice. I'm just trying to help you here. Have you two texted since last weekend?"

"Yeah," Ravi said. "It was pretty much Jessie telling me that she doesn't have time to meet up because she took a few extra shifts at her work-study job."

"Which is why you're here now on a Friday, brooding."

Ravi looked out at the crowd and rolled his eyes. Same shit, different day. There were the beer pong and card games, the groups of people talking. There was sexy dancing that would probably progress to make-out sessions and hooking up in one of the bedrooms upstairs. He had a lot of fun when he first started at university, but now he saw the parties as a desperate attempt for people to seize the freedom they could before they had to leave their college bubble.

"The good thing is Jessie's managed to keep your secrets safe. She hasn't bragged about all the things you've told her about yourself."

"She wouldn't do that," Ravi said. He'd shared more with Jessie than he'd shared even with Sahdna, and she knew as much as she did only because their families came from the same world.

Before Sahdna had a chance to respond, Deep and Vik strolled over from across the yard.

"It's good to finally see you out again," Vik said, and then cuffed Ravi's shoulder. "I feel like you haven't been around for the last month. You missed most of rush."

"I'm sure you all had it handled."

Deep chuckled as he scratched his thick beard. "We honest to god thought you had a thing for the first-year girl, and you were meeting her in secret or something. I saw her in the library a couple times this week when I was pulling stuff from my paper, and since you weren't there—"

"This week?" Ravi said, his spine straightening. "You saw her in the library this week?"

"Uh-oh," Sahdna said under her breath.

"Yeah," Deep said as he glanced over at Vik, then back to Ravi. "On the sixth floor. Isn't that where you were fighting over the same study room? We were actually looking for you when we saw her."

"Huh," Ravi said, his jaw clenching in response. "Yeah, I didn't realize she was in the room I usually take. She usually texts me . . ."

Vik held up his hands in surrender. "I thought you guys were just study-room enemies. Are we reading this wrong? Has the mighty Ravi fallen?"

"Oh my god, shut up," Sahdna said. She rolled her eyes. "The only person that Ravi is interested in is me." She wrapped an arm around Ravi's waist. "Babe, you want to get some pizza? I'm hungry."

"Come on," Deep said. "Sahdna, we know you've been hanging around with a first-year, too. Don't fuck with us."

Ravi felt Sahdna pinch his hip. "Ah, sorry, Vik. Sahdna's still my . . . uh, bestie. If she wants pizza, then she gets pizza."

"Did you just call her your bestie?" Deep asked.

"Bye," Sahdna said with a wave, and then began maneuvering Ravi toward the door.

"Thanks," he whispered against her temple.

Sahdna looked up at him. "Don't thank me yet. I'm about to say something that might piss you off. Ravi? If I was dating a girl who went out of her way to lie to me about our weekly meetings and then ended up studying in a different study room on the complete opposite end of the library, I'd want to know why."

"You're right," Ravi said. He stepped out onto the street and kept Sahdna close until a group of people walked by. "I should really go talk to her."

"You should," Sahdna said. "I'll walk with you a ways and then you can head toward the library."

"No, let me walk you back—"

"Or I'll catch a ride share," she said, holding up her hand like a traffic signal. "I don't need you to walk me all the way back to my house. It's at least twenty minutes from the library, if not more."

"Fine," Ravi said. They started toward the center of campus and Davidson Square. "Can I ask you something?"

"Shoot."

"Do you think it's ridiculous to date a first-year? I'll be gone in one more year, and she'll be left in this bubble where things like money and careers don't matter. She'll probably find another guy in a heartbeat and live out some ridiculously normal college romance that I can't give her. Not with my family."

"No," she said immediately. "I don't think dating a first-year is ridiculous. If she means enough to you, you'll make it work."

"But?"

"*But,*" she said, nudging him in the arm. "It won't be normal. You have to be willing to fight your family's expectations to take what you want. So be sure."

"You think I'm bad for Jessie," he said softly.

"There's no escaping your family legacy, Ravi. Your family is the poster child for tech success, so all eyes are on you and the legacy you represent. The world we live in is oppressive, and it's privileged, and there are so many problems with the way money flows in this weird, incestuous way in wealthy families, but you are the person they're turning to as the next generation to make it better."

The thought of hurting Jessie in any way was painful. Every moment they spent together was like a gift because he felt like he could be himself. He didn't hide who he was or what he did because he knew that she didn't really care. And if he was dishonest with her, she would be pissed off, because she only wanted the truth.

Sahdna tucked her hands in her pockets and waited expectantly, with one hip cocked to the side.

"Jessie is doing me a favor by ignoring me," he said.

Sahdna sighed. "Maybe? Only you can decide that."

He should go home. Jessie was giving him the easy way out, and he should take it. But he needed to talk to her one more time. He needed to tell her how he felt at least once.

Ravi took out his phone and pulled up their message history. What had started as short exchanges about when to meet about the letters included memes and videos now. It included long messages about a love story that was over fifty years old, and what they would do if they were Divya and Christian. It included their hopes and dreams and thoughts about their families.

He sent a quick note and received a response almost immediately.

RAVI: Hey, where are you?

JESSIE: Why?

RAVI: Just tell me where you are.

JESSIE: In my dorm.

RAVI: Okay, I'm coming to see you.

JESSIE: What the hell? No! It's a freshman dorm with a ton of Desis.

Sahdna leaned over his arm to look at the screen. "Oh yeah, you can't go over there, Ravi. Tanvi said that Jessie is really private, and if anyone spots you together in the dorm, they'll hound her out of curiosity, and I bet she's not used to that attention."

"I don't understand why people can't just mind their own business."

"Why, when it's way more fun paying attention to everyone else?" Sahdna said.

A car drove by and honked at them. Sahdna waved. She always smiled and waved whenever strangers approached her. It was part of what made her a great influencer. He used to be the same way, but he was so tired of sharing every part of his life with anyone who wanted it.

JESSIE: I'll meet you outside. I was going to Common Grounds to get a late-night boba, anyway.

RAVI: Be there in ten. I can't believe you were going to walk alone at night again. It's like you have a death wish.

JESSIE: I'll be fine. See you in ten.

"What are you going to tell her?" Sahdna asked when she saw Jessie's message.

Ravi wasn't sure. He knew that the best thing for Jessie was to break it off. They weren't dating, even though he spent more time with her than he had with anyone else in his three years on campus. "I don't know," he said.

She was waiting on the sidewalk for him when he reached the freshman towers. She wore a thick sweatshirt with the university logo on it, her face was freshly washed, and she was scrolling on her phone.

"Hi," he said as he approached her.

"Hi," she replied. "What are you doing here?"

"I think we should probably talk."

Before he could say another word, a group of students poured out of the freshman towers' front entrance. He turned his back to them and reached into his pocket for a vape like he always did. The only problem was he had quit, and as hungry as his urges were, he wasn't going back. All of his vapes were in a bowl sitting on his kitchen counter. The cartridges were mostly empty, and in the last few weeks, he hadn't gotten another one.

"Why don't we start walking toward Common Grounds?" Jessie said. "That way, we can just get it out of the way, and I can grab my boba."

They had taken a few steps in the direction of Lafayette Street, where the coffee shop was open late.

"What do you mean 'we can just get it out of the way'?" Ravi asked. He could feel his palms sweating, his heart pounding. He was way more nervous than he expected to be. Maybe because he knew that he was probably going to get rejected twice by the same woman.

She turned to face him now, her face illuminated by the streetlight. "I shouldn't have kissed you," she said in a rush. "I'm so sorry, I got caught up in the moment, and—"

"Why did you kiss me?" he asked.

"Because you're *you!*" she burst out. "Because you're actually a nice guy, even though you have every reason to be a self-centered asshole. Because you walk me home, even though you don't have to. And I bet you walk everyone else home, too, just because that's the kind of person you are. And because I really, really like you even though this is going nowhere, and—"

He took a step toward her, wrapped his arms around her waist, and lifted her on her toes. Then he leaned in and pressed a kiss to her mouth. It was as explosive and delicious as he remembered. The taste of her was as potent as a drug, and he couldn't get enough. Her mouth softened under his, and she wrapped her arms around his neck.

On the sidewalk, at night, in the chilly October evening, he felt safe with Jessie in his arms, and their mouths fused together.

When they pulled apart to catch their breath, Ravi rested his forehead against Jessie's and closed his eyes. "You're under my skin, Jessie Ahuja."

Her lips gently brushed his again as she spoke. "I have so much to lose, Ravi. We're doomed from the start. This can never work."

"It can while we're here," Ravi said. Then he kissed her again, this time deeper than the last. His tongue slipped inside her mouth, and she let out a small groan. Her fingers buried in the hair at the nape of his neck, and his hand tucked into the back pocket of her jeans. His body tensed in response to the way she strained against him.

"Hiding on the sixth floor doesn't change this," he said breathlessly when they pulled apart this time. They were pressed against each other, their arms pulling their bodies close and holding on like vises. He'd never felt like this before. Never wanted to feel like this before.

"I'm going to fall in love with you," she said, her voice shaking now, as if she was on the verge of tears. "I'm going to fall hard, and then we're going to hurt each other because we just don't make sense out in the real world. My family doesn't have the money yours does. I'll never go to fancy parties and fundraisers. I'll never meet the expectations of your parents. I'm not like Sahdna."

"None of that matters—"

"It does," she interrupted. "It does because if this gets in my head and it distracts me from my grades, I can lose my scholarship. I can lose sight of my goals. Of working extra hard to get the internship, and the job, and making the money to help my family so they don't have to work seven days a week. And if we do this anyway, despite the fact that we'll never have a future, my feelings for you will bruise and scar so deeply that I won't forget you until I'm far away from this place."

"You think that you won't hurt me the same way?" he burst out. "Jessie, I know that you have a lot to lose, but it wasn't until I met you that I started writing again. That I started dreaming. I am better because of you, and without you, I'll fade into the black-and-white world, the nonfiction existence that I had chosen to accept. But even with the possibility of this all going to shit, I'll take my chance." He then did something he had never done before. "Come back to my condo with me," he said. "Just . . . let's talk. I want to be with you. In your company. For as long as it lasts. And I promise you, no, I *swear* to you, that I will do everything I can to make sure that I support you in getting to your goals. I won't stand in your way, I'll be cheering you on. Because that's how important you are to me."

"I've never been with anyone," she whispered. Her eyes filling with tears. "I've never had the chance. Not just like this . . . but more. And god, Ravi, if I go back to your condo with you, I may want more. And then we'll just be even more complicated than we are."

He took a few even breaths at the thought of being naked with her, of holding her skin to skin and kissing the corners and grooves of her mouth, of her neck, of lacing his fingers through hers and pressing their joined hands against cool bedsheets. He knew that he'd been holding those images back for so long that he'd keep doing it if she wasn't ready. But he just wanted to be near her. That's what mattered. "If you're not ready, then I'll kiss you again, and walk you home," he said. He looked up at the freshman towers behind them. "Think about us. We're stronger than you think we are. I hope you trust me to believe that. And if you don't trust me tonight, then soon. Before school ends. No, before we finish reading the letters."

She was nodding before he even finished his sentence. "I trust you, Ravi. I trust you." There was a long pause; then her shoulders straightened. "Do you mean it?"

"Every word," he said immediately, then cocked his head and smiled. "But what are you talking about specifically?"

"That you'll . . . cheer me on. That we're stronger together."

"Of course," he burst out. "Can't you feel it?" He took her hand and placed it in the center of his chest. His heart beat strong and fast. It beat for her.

The feel and rhythm under her palm seemed to relax her even more. "This is hard for me. And everything I said, I meant. But I think you might be right, too."

"What are you saying?"

She leaned into his arms. "Take me to your condo, Ravi. I want to be with you."

He could feel his pulse racing. His need for her and his need to protect her both pulled at his heart. He was supposed to be thinking about an internship, about becoming another productive tech bro. But all he could think about in this moment was being with Jessie. It was fate from the start, and he had to wonder if Christian felt the same way before his love disappeared in a raging fire.

"Let's go, then," he whispered, and kissed her again. "Let's go."

SIXTEEN

Jessie

Jessie remembered listening to the girls in high school talk about their first time. She overheard conversations in the hall or on the bus. Kissing, then French kissing, then bases, like sex was a game. She'd been curious once, and at an Indian Association Diwali function in her town, she'd let one of the boys from another city who'd come to visit his grandparents touch her in the shadowed parking lot outside the Marriott banquet hall.

But this was different. This was Ravi, and she was both scared and excited to be with him. They walked in silence to his condo, with her hand gripped in his. She could feel the sweat from their nerves glue their skin together, but she didn't mind. When he squeezed her fingers in the elevator, Jessie knew that Ravi didn't mind, either.

They walked side by side down the hallway, her heartbeat pounding in her chest as they approached his door. He let them in, and together, they stepped inside, one foot in front of the other.

"Do you want to have something to drink?" he asked softly as he took off his shoes and flipped on the under-cabinet lights in his kitchen. The soft glow was enough to illuminate the space while also allowing the small downtown lights to shine through the windows.

"I'm okay, Ravi," she said as she toed off her shoes.

He watched her in the light of the condo, his voice hoarse. "You deserve romance."

She was caught off guard. "W-what?"

"Romance," he said as he took a step closer. "Roses, the words, a letter of your own. You deserve all of the sweetness that Divya got with Christian."

"I don't need that," Jessie said. She already felt lightheaded, dizzy with the possibilities of being with him.

"You do," Ravi replied. He reached out and touched her waist, then wrapped his arms around her to pull her close. Jessie breathed in his scent, took in the feel of his body as he whispered against her ear. "Because you believe in romance. You may want everyone to think that you're writing your paper about Divya Das so you can pass your seminar class. Because your grades are the most important thing to you. But you want Divya to have a happily ever after, too."

Jessie shivered as his lips grazed her neck. "People should know her name," she whispered. "They should know that even if she wasn't somebody important, her life still meant something."

Ravi's next move was so quick she didn't have time to anticipate it. He leaned down and scooped her up in his arms. "Ravi!"

He grinned boyishly, his expression free of the hard shield of sarcasm she'd come to expect. "Is this your first time?" he asked as she gripped his shoulders for balance.

Jessie nodded.

"Then let me give you as much romance as I can."

Her heart thrilled at the knowledge that he was doing this for her, and that he wanted her to have a good experience. Jessie rested her head against his shoulder and held him close as he carried her down the hall toward his bedroom. A king-size bed was made up with a white comforter and soft-blue pillows. Through the large windows, the lights of the city cast the room in a dreamy glow.

"Do you know the first thing I noticed about you?" Ravi said as he gently placed Jessie at the edge of the bed.

"What?"

"Your smell," he said softly.

She giggled. "You liked how I smelled?"

"Mm-hm," he said. He took off his hat and dropped it to the floor before reaching over his shoulder and yanking his sweatshirt and shirt off over his head. "You're sweet and warm, and I want to drink you up." His tanned chest was muscled and toned and covered with a thatch of chest hair that she wanted to touch.

So she did. She reached out and ran her fingers down the coarse curls that tapered to the waistband of his jeans.

"Jessie," he said, his voice low, rumbling with warning. "Let me romance you."

"I think you already have."

His laugh was husky now. He walked over to his dresser across from the foot of the bed and opened the top drawer. Jessie admired the wide set of his shoulders, his tapered waist, and the curve of his butt as he removed what looked like two condom packets before he returned to her side.

"Jessie, are you sure—"

"Ravi, just kiss me."

He dropped the condoms on the bedside table; then, cupping her face in his hands, he tilted her head up to his and pressed his lips against hers. A wave of electricity jolted her system.

Was this how it was always going to be? Would he always affect her this way? As he deepened the kiss, any doubt she had about him flew out the window.

Ravi's gripped her hips and lifted her further onto the pillows. He paused for a moment when his hands dropped to his belt buckle, as if waiting for her permission to move forward.

She nodded. "I want this," Jessie whispered. And then, lifting up on her elbows, she watched as he made quick work of pushing his jeans down his legs. He stood in his boxer briefs, his erection visible through the thin fabric.

Ravi put one knee on the bed and crawled toward her until she fell back against the mattress. He hovered over her for a moment, a breathless second, before his lips descended onto hers. Her fingers tunneled into his hair, and her legs spread to bracket his hips so that he fit against her more comfortably.

An ache grew between her legs and spread through her abdomen as she felt Ravi through her jeans. The hard lines of his legs, of his penis, and the weight of his chest pressed against hers. Her nipples came alive, and she felt like she was burning through her skin. She felt satisfied and needy at the same time.

Ravi tore his mouth away from hers, panting heavily. He took the edge of her shirt and quickly yanked it up over her head before lying back on top of her. His delicious weight anchored her to the bed and there was no one else she could see, nothing she could feel other than the softness of his body. They were skin to skin, and every nerve ending came alive with sensation as she stroked her hands down the broad, rigid muscles of his back.

He rolled to the side and shifted Jessie until she was on top, and together, with trembling fingers, they undid the clasp of her jeans. As she pushed them over her hips, she rocked forward until both of their sexes rubbed together.

They groaned, and Jessie felt an all-consuming need. "Ravi," she whispered, and, in silent communication, bucked her hips forward again.

He sat up, their lips meeting, and he quickly unclasped her bra so that he could rake his fingers over the sensitive peaks of her nipples. "Jessie," he groaned; then his lips covered one of her breasts, and her thoughts scattered.

At some point, he'd undone her ponytail, and with her long hair falling around them in a cascade of black waves, she closed her eyes, head tilted back, reveling in the feeling of being adored.

Then she was on her back again, and his mouth traced a line from breast to hip, until he pulled off her jeans and let them drop to the floor.

"Jessie?" she heard him say.

"Yes." He bent her knees, spread her thighs, and nudged her underwear out of the way. Ravi pressed a kiss against the soft heat of her vulva, his tongue licking at her wetness until she gasped and squirmed against the bed. His fingers gripped her thighs, holding her in place as he began to feast on her pleasure.

Jessie couldn't think, couldn't breathe as she felt the orgasm cresting inside her. She never imagined that she would feel this incredible, this worshipped by a man, especially one who at first seemed so arrogant. And then she couldn't think at all as the orgasm crashed through her, wrecking her until her body was taut and she was screaming his name in release. Her fingers tightened in his hair, her back arched off the bed, and she saw stars behind her eyelids.

They were both gasping for air as Ravi leaned back and grabbed a condom. He took off his boxer briefs, and in the glow of the city lights, she saw the thick length of him. She watched as he protected both of them by rolling on the condom.

He resumed his position between her legs, and distributed his weight to his forearms even as he dropped his forehead against hers.

"I want you so much," he whispered.

"I want you, too," she whispered back. He adjusted himself, and she felt the head of his erection notched at her opening.

"I don't want to hurt you."

Jessie squeezed her eyes shut, knowing that it would be impossible to avoid the pain, but that the pleasure would be worth it.

"I can take it," she whispered.

He pressed his lips against hers and slowly began rocking forward. One hand remained between them, and he found her clit with his thumb. He rubbed it in teasing circles, sending shock waves of pleasure through her body. Her hips rolled forward, and he buried himself deeper inside her until she felt the soft give, then a quick flash of pain. He was seated to the hilt.

She gasped against his mouth, and he swallowed it whole. Then with their fingers entwined, their hips began to move in slow, strong strokes. She could feel every part of him, rocking in and out, the ridges of his cock against the swollen wet heat of her vagina. With each thrust, the pleasure spiked, and she wanted to scream, wanted to beg for more as he let one hand go long enough to run it up her torso to cup her breast. Their bodies were damp now, covered in a thin sheen of sweat as they moved together in an achingly deep and slow rhythm.

"You're perfect," he panted as he thrust harder and harder. "You're so fucking perfect for me, Jessie."

She couldn't say anything, couldn't breathe anymore as he began to thrust into her, his patience fading to desperation. The sound of skin slapping reverberated through the room. Then, in a burst of light and ecstasy, she felt herself tumble over the edge and screamed out in release. Ravi pumped harder and faster, riding her orgasm until he, too, came.

Jessie wrapped her arms around Ravi as he collapsed against her, still firmly inside her body, pressing a kiss to his shoulder, the shell of his ear, his scruffy cheek, reveling in the hot, sticky sweat of his skin as his hands coasted over her body and curled under her arms.

"Ravi?" she whispered, her voice thready from the afterglow.

"Mm-hm?"

"You're perfect for me, too," she whispered. She felt his lips curve in a smile next to her, then felt the soft press of his mouth against her temple.

SEVENTEEN

Jessie

It was reckless, and absolutely wild to have sex with Ravi Kumar. But there she was, lying in bed for the second day in a row, wearing one of his shirts while playing with his hair as he rested his head on her stomach. His fingertips stroked her thighs, and the scruff of his jaw rubbed against the soft skin of her abdomen. Her first time had been perfect, and the second even better.

"We're supposed to be studying and reading more letters," she said. She felt drugged with sensation. Was this what it was like to be in love? Was this what people were so scared to find?

No, she thought. This was what people were so scared to lose. She had to prepare herself now because one day, this would be a memory and she'd have only the echoes of feeling to keep her comfortable at night.

"Read one," he said, his voice gruff as he continued to savor her, as if he couldn't have enough. She shifted, feeling the delicious soreness, the aches at the apex of her thighs from his touch. She felt different, but the same all at once.

Jessie reached to the left to grab the book she'd brought to bed and flipped open the cover, where the letters were neatly stacked in chronological order. She picked up the next letter and unfolded it. With her fingers carelessly running through Ravi's hair, she began to read the letter aloud.

"'Dear Jaan, today, I was caught slipping my letter into your book. I stood in the kaleidoscope room, early in the morning before anyone else came to study, and had reached the second level when Gayatri Singh entered, calling my name. She's been my best friend since we began at the university, and I had to tell her why I was in the tower.'"

Jessie froze, her entire body tensing just as Ravi's did the same. He sat back on his knees, shirtless, with only a pair of boxers on. His eyes were wide as he glanced back and forth between Jessie and the letter.

"Did you say Gayatri Singh?"

"I did," Jessie said. She handed him the letter.

"Gayatri Singh," he said softly. "It says here that Divya asked her to help keep their secret, which Gayatri promised to do. We have a name."

"We have a name," Jessie said. "Oh my god. If we find this person, maybe we can verify whether or not Divya's story is the one that became campus legend. What do you think?"

Ravi carefully put the letter aside, then, with a grin, pulled Jessie into his arms so that she sat on his thighs and wrapped her legs around his waist. "I think we should go and find Gayatri Singh," he said, then kissed her until they were both breathless again.

"In a minute," she whispered as they both lay back onto the rumbled sheets. "We need a minute."

It took a few hours before they were up, showered, dressed, and ready to find Gayatri Singh. Jessie was so glad she'd saved the yearbook archives, which made it easier to look up her records.

"Edison, New Jersey," Ravi said, reading the computer screen from over Jessie's shoulder. "Great. That makes it infinitely harder to find her. Why can't she be from some remote town in the Midwest?"

"Because Gayatri Singh couldn't thrive in the Midwest back in 1972."

They started with Facebook and began reviewing the Gayatris that followed the university page. There were over fifty, and some of them had pictures of their kids or pets as their profile image, which made it impossible to identify their likeness to a yearbook photo from the seventies.

"This is going to take forever," Jessie said.

Ravi pressed a kiss to the crown of her head. "We have time."

She paused at his words. Why did they feel like a reference to their relationship instead of a complicated search for Divya Das's friend? She'd have to tuck that thought away for later.

He rounded the island and opened his fridge, perusing its sparse contents, while she watched him out of the corner of her eye, continuing to scroll through her laptop. That's when a face that looked oddly familiar appeared on her screen.

"Is that you, Gayatri?" she murmured as she clicked on the profile. The details that appeared were limited, since this Gayatri Singh had kept her information private. But there were a few photos that she was able to see, one of them from a hospital picnic six months ago.

Jessie followed the information trail until she found the hospital's social-media account and scrolled until she found the picnic. There was a photo of a pretty South Asian woman surrounded by children, perhaps her grandchildren. Her hair was streaked with orange and white. She wore traditional Punjabi clothes.

But there was something in her eyes. Jessie cleaned closer. "Oh my god," she whispered. "I think I found her."

Ravi came around the counter and looked at the side-by-side images Jessie had pulled up on the screen: the blurry black-and-white photo from the yearbook and the color image of a woman fifty years older.

"I think that's her, Jessie," Ravi said. "I mean, there's a good chance it's not, and the woman we're looking for doesn't even know how to operate a computer, but she might be the one. Is there a way you can reach out to her? Through email or something?"

Jessie checked her contact fields, which were all blank. But she was able to check to see if she followed her children.

"There," she said, and then tapped the screen at the family connections. "Her daughter is on Facebook and has a public profile. She's in her early forties. Do you think she'd mind if we reached out to her about her mother's connection at the university?"

"We might as well try," Ravi said. "Do you want me to send the message? I can use my name."

Jessie took a minute to think about the potential impact of using Ravi's name. The woman was older, so there was a chance that a tech conglomerate family name didn't resonate with her, but it was worth a shot.

She twisted in her chair and looked up at Ravi. "Do you think you could ask her for an interview for a story you're working on or something? I don't want to scare her away by mentioning a school project."

"Sure," Ravi said, then dropped a kiss on the tip of Jessie's nose. It was amazing how easy it felt to be with him this way. His touch was the most natural feeling to her now that they'd been together, and she wanted more of it. It felt comforting to her, and the imprint of his fingertips were reminders of how delicious he made her feel.

"Okay," Jessie said. "Let's message Gayatri Singh and see if she's willing to talk to us. Edison, New Jersey, isn't too far from here, so if she won't chat on the phone, then it won't be too difficult to rent a car or something and drive out to see her."

"Let's do it now, then," Ravi said. "Then we should get some homework done. Not that I don't want to spend the rest of the night with you; it's just that I don't want to be the reason your grades slip after you've been working so hard."

Her cheeks warmed. "Thanks," she said. "I care about your grades, too."

EIGHTEEN

Jessie

The last thing Jessie expected was for Gayatri Singh to agree to an in-person meeting at her daughter's chai café in Edison, New Jersey. She wasn't going to turn down the opportunity, though. It was too good to pass up.

Because Jessie wasn't the strongest driver, Ravi manned the red Lexus they'd borrowed from one of his friends. Jessie was still unsure of whether it was a good idea for them to borrow the expensive car, but they couldn't secure a rental like they had planned on such short notice.

"Are you sure you're not upset?" Ravi asked for the tenth time as they pulled into the parking lot of the chai café.

"No," she said again. "It was my fault I forgot that I had a shift this morning, not yours."

She saw his jaw tense, and she knew that he didn't believe her after all the times she told him how important her job was to her. But she had no one to blame but herself. And it was hard to feel guilty when she was so happy. She would've probably been in worse shape if her manager weren't so understanding. Luckily, she was able to trade a shift at the last minute with someone else who desperately needed the free time on a Tuesday night.

"I don't want to get in the way of your work," he said as he nosed the car into a parking spot and shut off the engine. "I promised you I'd be supportive."

With more confidence than she ever thought she'd possess, Jessie cupped his cheek. She enjoyed the rush she felt when he leaned into her touch. "I'll let you know if you get in the way," she said.

"Good," he replied.

They both got out of the car at the same time and headed toward the front door. Before she reached the café entrance, she felt Ravi step up beside her, then slip his hand in hers. Their palms pressed together, and their fingers interlaced. She looked up at him and smiled even as he opened the door for her to walk through first.

"Jessie Ahuja?"

Jessie turned to look at the slender woman in a dark-maroon shirt and khakis step in front of their path. She folded her hands together and nodded so rapidly that Jessie worried her head would bobble off her neck.

"That's me," Jessie said. "Hi, you must be Gayatri Auntie's daughter? The one we've been emailing with?"

She nodded again. "I can take you to see my mother. She hasn't been this excited for visitors in a while."

Jessie looked back at Ravi, who grinned. She was glad that he came along and was willing to flex his family name to get into the good graces of a woman in her early seventies.

They followed Gayatri's daughter toward the back of the restaurant, where they turned a corner and stopped in front of a booth with brown leather bench seats and a glossy hardtop table. Seated on one side of the booth was an elegant older woman with rich black hair, dressed in a matching pantsuit and stylish red glasses. Engrossed in a game of Candy Crush, she briefly looked up when she saw them approach and smiled as bright as a sunbeam. Her gaze locked directly onto Ravi.

"I love your father's website. It's the best way to talk to my family in India."

"Thank you so much. It's lovely to meet you." He leaned down to press a kiss against her papery cheek. "We appreciate that you're taking the time out of your day to answer some questions."

Gayatri giggled like a schoolgirl; then her eyes met Jessie's, and her smile warmed. "You want to talk about Divya."

"I do," Jessie said. "Can we sit with you?"

"Sure, sure."

Her accent carried the faintest hint of India, noticeable in the hard consonants and rounded vowels. She'd graduated from the New Jersey Technology Center two years after Divya disappeared, then went on to marry one of her classmates, who, like both their fathers, became a physician.

Jessie slipped into the booth opposite Gayatri. Ravi's thigh brushed hers as he settled next to her.

"Let's get some chai," Gayatri said. She motioned to her daughter and spoke in rapid Punjabi, the words harder and faster than the soft English she'd used to greet them. Her daughter nodded and slipped into the back room.

"Now," she said, folding her aged hands in front of her on the table. Her nails were painted the same shade of red as her glasses. "What do you want to know?"

"We are writing this story for a class," Jessie said, "but we actually have some information that we didn't share in our email because we weren't sure if it was something you knew about." She reached into her small cross-body bag and withdrew the first letter that she'd read with Ravi. Gayatri's expression shifted into one of shock and dismay.

"Where did you get that?" she whispered as she took the letter out of Jessie's hand. Her eyes began to water. "It's been over fifty years, and I can still recognize these ridiculous letters on powder-blue paper."

Ravi rested a hand on Jessie's knee under the table and squeezed. It was as if he knew exactly what she needed to calm her racing heart. "We were playing a game," she said. "A ridiculous one. We went into Davidson Tower, which has been locked in preparation for the renovation, and we found a desk on the second floor that looked like it survived the fire."

"You found the secret drawer," Gayatri whispered.

Jessie's heart began to pound. "You knew about the letters."

Gayatri Singh's daughter returned with a tray of chai cups and papad. As much as Jessie was eager to try the crispy wafer snack, she was desperate for answers. It had been weeks since they read the first letter, and even though they'd made progress in painting a picture of what happened to Christian and Divya, it wasn't enough.

Gayatri wrapped her hands around the cup and picked it up with trembling hands to take a sip. When she put it back in the saucer, it looked like some of the lines around her mouth had softened. She glanced at the letter between them, then back at Jessie.

"I knew about the letters after Divya had already fallen in love with Christian."

"Do you remember Christian's last name?" Ravi asked.

"Of course I do," Gayatri said, her tone bitter. "He was the president's son, after all. His name is probably all over the university buildings by now."

Not just a person with privilege and power, Jessie thought. But the president himself.

"Hastings," Ravi added. "Divya Das was in love with Christian Hastings."

Gayatri nodded, her face grim. "I was sworn to secrecy, and I've kept up my end of the bargain for over fifty years. But President Hastings died a few years back, and I feel like I can speak more freely now."

"We were right," Ravi said softly. "They *were* the source of the campus legend."

"Of course," Gayatri said softly. "That's all people could talk about for weeks, then months. But by the time I graduated, people barely remembered Divya's and Christian's names. And those of us who knew Divya and Christian preferred to keep it that way."

164

"Why?" Ravi asked. "Why not memorialize your friends' love story?"

"Because times were different back then. We learned very quickly that we were not welcome in this country. And to be in love with someone who is White? There was a lot of discussion about it after that big law case."

"Law case?" Ravi asked.

"*Loving v. Virginia,*" Jessie said quietly. She turned to Ravi. "*Loving v. Virginia* was decided in 1967, less than five years before Divya and Christian met." It seemed so inconsequential now. Interracial relationships were normal.

"And it didn't just apply to Black and White families," Gayatri said, her accent from decades past hardening her words. "We weren't impacted to the same extent, but it still affected my friends and loved ones. In the end, I don't know if there was a happily ever after for Divya and Christian. And they wanted their relationship to be kept a secret. As a friend, I felt like I should honor their wishes."

Jessie had so many questions. She couldn't stop thinking about the order in which she planned on asking them on the drive to Edison. But now, there was only one that came to mind.

"Can you tell us what Divya Das was like?" she asked.

Gayatri's expression softened. "It's been a long time, but I can still remember how beautiful she was. Her family was very strict. Stricter than mine. But she was still so curious and wanted to try everything. She hoped to be a teacher. It would've been the perfect job for her."

Setting her cup down, Jessie fought back the tremor in her hands, not wanting to reveal how deeply moved she was by the revelation that this person knew precious information about the woman they'd been trying to learn about for so long. Divya wanted to be a teacher. Her family was strict. She was as beautiful in real life as she was in her picture. It was no longer a mere story; it had transformed into tangible history before their eyes.

"We haven't read all of the letters yet, Auntie," Ravi said. "But we do know that the latest one was dated in November of 1972. Do you know what happened to Divya and Christian?"

"I do," Gayatri Singh said, her voice tinged with bitterness. "Divya wasn't the only person from her family to be accepted into the program. Her cousin Vaneeta was also a student. Vaneeta and Divya grew up together. Their fathers were brothers and were able to immigrate to the States at the same time. Vaneeta was always jealous of Divya's accomplishments. They were in constant competition since they were children. At least that's the way I saw it.

"Divya and Christian were in the library, in an embrace. That's when Vaneeta found them. I think she followed her cousin, suspecting she was up to something. It took no time at all for that snake to run home and tell Divya's parents."

The hot masala tea scorched Jessie's mouth. "Auntie, did Divya and Christian run away?"

Gayatri didn't answer right away, as if she were still grieving the loss of her friend.

Maybe there was a part of Jessie that thought Divya and Christian had their happily ever after. But the sadness etched across Gayatri's face made this seem like an impossibility. Her teacup trembled. "The next day, Divya came to school crying. She was going back to India. She was getting married. That's what all of our parents expected from us in those days. She said that the next day she was going to run away with Christian before her parents got to the university. They were going to take what little money they had managed to hide and start over somewhere else."

Ravi's grip tightened on Jessie's thigh and she covered his hand with hers.

Gayatri continued. "The plan was absolutely ludicrous. Women, especially Indian women, didn't have power back in the seventies. We constantly fought against a system that never acknowledged us as anything more than charity. I was afraid for Divya, and I told her that.

What if Christian gave up on her? She'd have no one. But I hugged her, and I gave her whatever pocket money I had available to me. Then she went to the library, and I never saw her again. That night, there was a fire in Davidson Tower. I always wondered . . ."

They were quiet for a long time. Jessie knew there was always a possibility that Divya and Christian set the fire intentionally as a distraction, but it was sounding more and more like what had actually happened. They could've hurt so many other people in the library that night. Did the means justify the ends?

Ravi nudged her in the arm. "Jessie, I just realized something."

She shook her head as if clearing the brain fog. "What is it?"

"What if we look at some of the faculty? They might have been students at the time the fire happened. The newsletter always brags about the retention rate of graduates who come back and teach. Professor Barnard might even be—"

"Barnard?" Gayatri said. "Lydia Barnard?" Her eyes sharpened. "I know her . . ."

Jessie's heart pounded, the same way it had when she'd first seen the letters. She looked up at Ravi, whose mouth was set in a thin line.

"We should probably take advantage of those office hours," he said.

Gayatri Singh made a soft sound of understanding, and Jessie turned away from Ravi to look in her direction.

"I understand now," she said softly. Her finger, curled at the knuckle, motioned back and forth between both of them. "You two. You are together."

"We are," Ravi said, his voice resolute.

"But you're going back to your family, and Jessie is staying here," Gayatri added. Her face had such sadness in it, such understanding as she looked at Jessie.

"We don't know yet," Jessie said softly.

"Well, I hope you learn from Divya and Christian," she said.

"Excuse me?" Jessie asked.

The woman's pain was reflected in the glassy surface of her eyes. "Divya and Christian sacrificed their family and friends for each other. If they really found happiness, they would've come back to us. But they never did."

"You think they died," Ravi said softly.

Gayatri nodded. She looked every bit her age now because of the deep lines around her mouth, and the exhaustion etched in her frail frame. "I learned a lot from my education here, but the one piece of advice I still try to follow is something Divya's story taught me. You can't find meaning in someone else's happiness. You have to find meaning in your own. I hope the sacrifices you'll make are worth the fleeting joy you have now."

With that omen hanging over her head, Jessie drank her chai.

APRIL 2, 1972

Dear Jaan,

You didn't come to the kaleidoscope room today. I fear that our love story may be coming to an end, and it's better that we take some time apart.

NINETEEN

Jessie

Jessie loved her job behind the information desk, but she hated
that it took away time from finding out more about the letters.
Now their quest was stalled because they wouldn't be able to see
Professor Barnard until the next day.

Ravi seemed to take it in stride. His argument about taking a break
and focusing on their real lives for a few days seemed like a good idea. It
allowed her time to process and to take an extra shift at the information
desk. Ravi, who always seemed to finish his homework quickly and efficiently, had bought a new thriller from one of his favorite writers and
said that he'd come and read in the student center until she finished.

She didn't know why his love of literature shocked her so much.
He preferred thrillers and mysteries and horror, but occasionally picked
up graphic novels and romances as well. Once Jessie started asking him
about the stories he liked, Ravi could talk for hours. He'd tell her about
his favorites, the plot holes that he wished the writers would address,
and the new releases he was looking forward to.

Jessie checked her phone when she received an incoming text
message.

RAVI: Sorry I'm running late! I know I said I'd come and read in
the student center today, but I got sidetracked. Be there soon.

Jessie sent a thumbs-up emoji, then looked down at her physics homework again. She'd excelled in all her midterms, but she needed to keep her grades up through the rest of the semester if she wanted to start off strong. It was just that one seminar class that had her worried.

She glanced up at the sound of the student-center doors opening, then stiffened when she saw Sahdna and Tanvi walk in together. They both wore spandex workout sets and carried water bottles with their key-card wallets.

"Hi!" Tanvi said as she approached the information desk. She crossed her arms and leaned against the ledge. "Busy day?"

Jessie held up her physics book. "Brutal." She loved physics, and sometimes doing the assignments calmed her at night, but it did take a lot of concentration and work.

"I know you said that you were almost done with your shift," Tanvi added. "How about playing hooky from the library today and coming to yoga with us? You liked it last week!"

"I did," Jessie admitted. Tanvi had demanded she take a break and spend some time in the gym. They were over the halfway mark in their first semester of college, and it was clear that Tanvi was her only close friend on campus while the rest of her classmates remained at a safe distance so they didn't distract her from her classes. But like Ravi, Tanvi refused to stay at arm's length, and now they were friends, and that meant Jessie was dedicated to cultivating their relationship just as much as she was dedicated to everything else that was important in her life.

But right now, under Sahdna's watchful eye, and with Ravi's texts popping up on her phone, she had no choice but to say no. "Unfortunately, I have plans."

"We saw Ravi on the way here," Sahdna said, as if reading her mind. "He mentioned you guys were doing something."

Jessie looked at her phone. "Oh? Where was he?"

Sahdna pointed to the glass doors. "We were at the frat house because I wanted to use their deck for a video series I'm shooting, and he had just stopped by to talk to Vik and Deeps. He said he'll be right behind us."

"Great," she said, trying not to smile. She knew that Sahdna and Ravi were friends, but were they close enough that he would tell her about their relationship? For the last few weeks, they had managed to convince everyone that they were just friends, but Sahdna and Ravi were close.

"What were they talking about at the frat house?" Tanvi asked.

Sahdna shrugged. "The guys asked him for his help, and he's such a nice guy, he probably couldn't say no. When we were leaving, I think they making summer vacation plans. Ravi was arguing about this internship he's supposed to do with his dad or his brother."

Jessie stiffened at the mention of an internship.

Tanvi cocked her head. Jessie was pretty sure she was completely oblivious to the tension that existed between her new girlfriend and her roommate. "I know this is, like, super privileged for me to think," Tanvi said as she lowered her voice and leaned closer across the desk, "but I thought we got to a point where families pressuring their children to enter specific careers was no longer a thing. Is Ravi really fighting with his parents about an internship that most people in his shoes would die for?"

"I doubt the fight is about South Asian expectations," Sahdna said.

"No, I think it *is* a little bit about being South Asian," Jessie said. "His family had to work to be the powerhouse it is today. It adds a whole layer of importance to what Ravi is turning down. Or better yet, what he thinks he can accomplish on his own with his wri—er, his media studies major."

Sahdna pursed her lips.

"I'm sure he'll figure it out," Tanvi said. "He's still a Kumar, right?"

"Right," Jessie said. She hoped that her roommate was right.

"So what are you guys working on?" Tanvi asked, turning back to Jessie. "Some group project or something?"

Jessie wanted desperately to tell Tanvi everything. She knew that even though Tanvi was bubbly and cheerful all the time, she was incredibly smart. She constantly scored the top of her class and had even helped Jessie with math homework the day before. Hopefully when they figured out the letters, she could buy Tanvi dinner and gush about the whole story.

But for now, she remained evasive. "It's something like that," she said.

"Here comes that Kumar now," Sahdna said when the doors of the student center opened. Jessie looked up, warming at the sight of Ravi walking in with his backpack slung over one shoulder, a thick university sweatshirt fitted to his toned frame. His hair was starting to grow a little long, and curls peeked out from under the rim of his signature backward hat.

He smiled when he saw Jessie, then waved at Sahdna and Tanvi. "Hey, I told you I was right behind you," he said.

Jessie wasn't sure how they were supposed to greet each other now that they were together. Her fingers trembled as she ran them down the page of the physics textbook in front of her. "Hi," she said.

In a move that both surprised and delighted her, Ravi gripped the ledge of the desk, hoisted himself up so he could lean over, and planted a noisy kiss at the corner of her mouth. "Hello, gorgeous," he said.

She could feel the heat rising in her cheeks. "I heard that you were visiting your friends at the frat house."

"I was," he said. He looked back and forth between Jessie, Sahdna, and Tanvi. "Vik is on student government. They're involved in providing student feedback for the tower renovation, and he needed help with his presentation. I also wanted to see if he knew anything about what was going on."

"It's a shame that they're going to take down all of that stained glass," Tanvi said.

Jessie nodded. "I feel the same way."

"Actually," Ravi said slowly, "there's a good chance they might not do it anymore. They still have to convert the tower into more computer space, because there's just not enough on campus and in the library, but after talking with Vik, he said I might be able to use my name to convince the renovation committee to keep a part of it."

Jessie's mouth dropped. "Are you serious?"

He nodded, and the corner of his mouth curved up in a half smile that made her stomach flutter. "My father is always looking for ways to be philanthropic that will make him look good. A big-ass donation should do the trick. What do you think?"

"I think that's amazing," she said. Her voice shook at the thought of being able to see the kaleidoscope room and its full glory after the renovations were complete. "But why?"

"Because of you," he said. "And because of me. If that room was powerful enough to bring two people together like that, shouldn't it be memorialized?"

"Yeah," she said, then cleared her throat.

The alarm on her phone went off, breaking the tension. "Ah, my shift is over. Maybe we can celebrate or something. Even if it's not a done deal, I feel like that's good enough for truffle fries."

"I love the truffle fries at Rothby's!" Tanvi said. She pressed her hands against her stomach, then turned to Sahdna. "Babe. Maybe we can go to a later class and join them for truffle fries instead?"

"I'd actually really like to go to the class," Sahdna said.

"Ugh, I know you're right, but those truffle fries."

Sahdna laughed and squeezed Tanvi's arm. "After. Jessie, Ravi, we'll see you guys later!"

"See you later, roomie," Tanvi called out cheerfully as Sahdna dragged her out the front door. Then Ravi and Jessie were alone again.

"So, truffle fries?" Ravi asked.

"Yeah," she said. She shook off the icy coldness from Sahdna's presence and logged out of the computer at her desk. "Truffle fries."

TWENTY

Ravi

Ravi knew that it was probably a bad idea to go to the professor who was grading their final papers and ask her if she had anything to do with Davidson Tower in her youth. But he realized now more than ever that when Jessie put her mind to something, there was no holding her back.

"We don't have to bring her in on this," he said for the hundredth time that morning. "I'm sure we can find the same answers on our own."

She tugged on the oversized sweatshirt she wore that she'd taken from his closet. She said that his clothes always felt better than her own. "Ravi, if there is a chance she can give us a single puzzle piece, then I want to ask for it. She was *there*. Gayatri remembered her so clearly, so she had to know Divya."

Ravi led Jessie down the empty corridor on the fourth floor of Hastings Hall, the floor that housed the offices for the professors and the graduate students. Professor Barnard's office was located at the end of the wing.

As they approached the office door, Ravi took a deep breath and stepped back so Jessie could enter first. He watched her read the quotes on the glass: One from Shakespeare. One from Zora Neale Hurston.

And a poem from Charles Simic. Jessie lifted her fist and knocked gently against the Simic poem.

There was the sound of papers being shuffled inside before Professor Barnard called out, "Come in!"

Jessie turned to Ravi and nodded before twisting the doorknob and entering. Professor Barnard's office was the shape of a rectangle, with large windows stretching from the floor to the twelve-foot-high ceiling. Along one wall was a row of bookshelves crammed with hardcovers, paperbacks, mass-market paperbacks, spiral-bound books, leather-bound books, and stacks of paper held together with binder clips. There were also framed photos of children, one of Disney World, where Professor Barnard stood next to an attractive older man. They wore a set of matching Mickey and Minnie ears on a black headband. In front of the window and adjacent to the bookshelves was a low-back couch.

Professor Barnard sat on the opposite side of the windows closest to the door. She reclined in a leather office chair in front of a pristinely organized white desk. Her computer monitor took up most of the surface space. There was also a lamp that gave off a soft yellow glow, a small succulent, and a mouse pad with a green mouse that matched the green keyboard.

"Ravi and Jessie from my nonfiction seminar," she said in greeting. Her lips curled at the corners. Serene. Practical. Practiced. "How can I help you two? I admit, most students don't use my office hours unless it's exam season. They almost never come together, either."

Ravi sat down on the couch, then turned to Jessie, who did the same. "We were working on the paper for the final," he said. "Professor Barnard, we know a lot of students in the class are writing about the campus legend surrounding Davidson Tower."

"Yes, I do believe that's a popular subject."

"We both decided to choose the same topic."

She raised her brow skeptically.

It's too late to back out now.

Jessie pressed her knees together, then rested them against Ravi's thigh. He wanted to reach out and hold her hand.

"Professor Barnard," she began. "We started to do some digging into the legend of Davidson Tower. And I think, with the help of some information that fell into our laps, we've been able to find the couple that's thought to have disappeared."

Professor Barnard's shoulders tensed, but her easy smile told a different story. She clasped her hands and rested them on her knees. "What information makes you believe that?"

Jessie looked over at Ravi, and he nodded at her.

"We know their names," Jessie said.

Professor Barnard's jaw clenched slightly. "I have to admit, I think you're the first students to ever come to me and claim that you know the name of the legendary couple in my twenty years of teaching."

"You were a student in the university at the time she was alive," Ravi said. He glanced down at Jessie. "I think you may have known Divya Das."

There was that strange stillness again in Professor Barnard's demeanor. "Divya Das? Yes, it rings a bell, but I admit it's been a long time. I could be imagining it at my age. I may have gone to school with a Divya Das. But how can you be so sure that's the person the legend is based on?"

"We spoke to Divya's best friend at the time," Ravi continued, "and she said that only a handful of people knew the truth about what happened to Divya and Christian that night. She had some pretty convincing stories."

Professor Barnard stiffened at the mention of Christian's name. "We discussed reliable narrators and resources in class last week. You'll have to provide ample evidence if someone claims to be friends with—"

She stopped midsentence when she saw the blue letter that Jessie slowly retrieved from her bag. Her pallor became even more pronounced.

"They wrote letters to each other and hid them in the library," Jessie said. "Ravi and I have read most of the ones we uncovered. The last letter we combed through named another South Asian student who caught Divya and Christian together."

Professor Barnard flinched. "Where did you find those letters in the library?" she said. "And how do you know that they're accurate?"

This was where it got tricky. If they admitted that they were in Davidson Tower when it was locked up for the renovation project, then there was a good chance that they'd get in trouble. There was also a chance that Professor Barnard might shut down any access to the library for both Jessie and Ravi in fear that they might find something else, something they weren't allowed to see.

In an effort to distract her, Ravi took the envelope from Jessie and stood. He crossed the room and handed it to Professor Barnard to read. There was a slight tremble in her grip, the barest intake of breath. She opened the envelope, then began reading. When she was finished, she pressed the paper closed and handed it back to Ravi, as if she never wanted to see it again.

Ravi sat back down next to Jessie, who rested a hand over his knee. Her tension was as palpable as their professor's. "The letters are dated, and there's information in them that corresponds with all of the events, the rumors and the stories about the missing students from the 1972 fire. When we tracked down Divya's college friend, she verified the handwriting and said that it felt as familiar as her own because Divya loved to write letters to all of her family and friends. Professor Barnard, we're just trying to find—"

"The truth behind the names?" Professor Barnard raised an eyebrow as if the very idea was ridiculous. Her fingers trailed over the crisp line of her pants. "You two have gotten further than anyone. For that, I applaud you."

"But?" Ravi said. He could feel it coming from a mile away. His parents were big fans of this phrase structure.

"But," Professor Barnard continued, "there are certain stories that aren't ours to tell."

"What makes a story something that we don't have the right to tell? We found the letters. Can't we write about them from our perspective? We want to give respect to a name that's been lost over time."

Professor Barnard was already shaking her head. "Divya and Christian's story is so much bigger than you may think. They deserve peace. If you want to write about something you found in the library that may or may not be connected to their narrative, then that's your prerogative. But you have to ask yourself why." She straightened her suitcoat, then stood. "Now most student papers are about the Davidson family that donated the money for the tower back in the forties. I suggest you stick to that name instead. I'm so sorry to cut our conversation short, but I have a faculty meeting to get to. Good effort. Let me know if you'd like to discuss another topic, and I'd be happy to see you again during office hours."

Ravi stood, Professor Barnard's words circling in his head like vultures. When Jessie looked like she was ready to argue with her, he shook his head. "Thanks, Professor Barnard. We'll see you in class."

He waited until they'd stepped outside of her office and walked hand in hand some distance down the hall before he turned to her. "She knows more than we thought. She's got to be connected to the story directly, but how is that even possible?"

"I don't know," Jessie said with a frustrated sigh. "Why did you want to leave? We could've pressed her for information. She stonewalled us."

Ravi's heart continued to thud hard and fast in his chest. "That's not true. She did give us some information. Inadvertently."

"And what would that be?" Jessie asked, tilting her head.

"Professor Barnard was speaking in the present tense," he said. "As if Divya Das and Christian are still very much part of the same story."

Jessie's eyes widened. "Oh my god. She was."

"We have to finish reading the letters and put together all the puzzle pieces."

Jessie stopped and faced him, their fingers still entwined. "But what if Professor Barnard is right?" she said, worrying her bottom lip between her teeth. "What if this story isn't one for us to tell?"

He wasn't sure why she would have doubts now. She had wanted to figure out the truth so badly that she had rummaged through Davidson Tower after his friends locked her in there, taking it as an opportunity to explore instead of freaking out like any normal person would.

Ravi leaned down so he could press his forehead against hers. "What's changing your mind? Professor Barnard's warning?"

She shrugged. "This was always so much more than a grade to me, but something about the way she warned us off makes me think I don't have the right to do this."

"You do," Ravi said. He didn't know why he felt so anxious about the thought of her giving up, especially since he hadn't understood her obsession in the first place. But her hesitation worried him. "Jessie, you've put in so much work already. You can't stop now. Worst-case scenario, this was all a hoax. Best-case scenario? They caused a small fire where no one else was hurt, and they ran away to live happily ever after."

She pulled back, but not far enough that he couldn't feel her soft breath coasting over his lips. "I guess I'm scared of what I'll find. Especially if they're not together."

"Why is that?" Ravi asked.

"Because what if they realized they were a mistake and decided to part ways? Their cultures were so different, and their actions shattered the trust of everyone around them. Was a college romance really worth sacrificing their entire worlds?"

Ravi didn't know how to answer that. He'd never found anything worth fighting for. He wondered if Christian and Divya felt like they were fighting for each other, too. He stepped back, and his fingers fell away from Jessie's. There was a small space between them now.

"Come on," he said. "We can't let fear stop us from facing the inevitable."

Even if the inevitable had the power to break his heart into tiny shards.

He'd never related to Divya Das's words more.

TWENTY-ONE

Jessie

Jessie had a hard time falling asleep after their meeting with Professor Barnard. Ravi could probably see the stress on her face and had asked her to pack a bag and spend the night at his condo so they could try to process what they had learned together.

Thankfully, it was easier to fall asleep in his bed, comforted by the sound of Ravi's easy breathing as he read a book by the soft glow of the small lamp on his bedside table. The gentle rustling of pages and the soothing hum of the ceiling fan provided the steady rhythm she needed to find solace and dreams.

She must have sensed his absence, the cold emptiness in the bed beside her, which is what woke her in the middle of the night. The blackout curtains engulfed the room in darkness, so she felt the bed next to her to find Ravi, only to touch sheets that were cool against her fingertips.

"Ravi?" she whispered as she sat up, the sheets pooling at her waist. She wore one of his old T-shirts, and the thin fabric wasn't enough to keep her warm in the late-fall chill.

When her vision adjusted, she saw a light under the bedroom door, and she slipped out of bed and crossed the room to see where he had gone.

The under-cabinet lights in the kitchen glowed, and the TV hummed softly with the sounds of an old TV sitcom. Ravi sat on the couch, his laptop resting on his knees with a Word document open. As she approached, he looked over his shoulder.

"Hey," he said softly. "Did I wake you?"

"Sort of," she said as she rounded the couch. She grabbed the throw blanket from the ottoman and sat at his side so he could wrap an arm over her shoulders. She shook out the throw and covered both of them with it to ward off the chill. "You were gone."

She felt a kiss against her brow, and a warm feeling spread across her chest.

"I had an idea for this story I'm writing," he said softly. "I wanted to get it down before I forgot."

"Mm-hm," Jessie said. Sleep was starting to invade her senses again. "Do you want me to leave you alone for a bit so you can work on it?"

"No, I think I'm done," he said.

He minimized the window, and a browser screen with a list of job titles popped up. She saw the words *research and development* in bold letters under one of the titles.

"I don't mean to pry," she said, shifting to an upright position. "But why are you looking at jobs?"

Ravi slid his hand off her shoulders and down her arm before he tapped the screen. "They're not jobs," he said. "They're internships."

Jessie remembered Sahdna mentioning that he was discussing internships with his friends. It stung that he hadn't talked to her about it earlier.

"My brother had my father's chief of staff send me this list," Ravi continued. "They want me to choose something for the summer at one of their companies. I still would have to interview for it, but they've made it clear that I'd be a shoo-in."

It was on the tip of her tongue to call out the nepotism of the situation. The likelihood of someone like her ever getting recognized by an HR department at one of those companies was next to impossible, and here he was, interviewing for jobs.

"I know how it sounds," he said ruefully. "And I recognize how privileged this makes me. Here I am, walking right into a position when someone in your shoes would have to interview and fight to be seen."

"But?" she said as she shifted on the couch. The throw was still tucked around her shoulders. "What's on your mind?"

"The thing is I . . . I don't want to become an engineer." He let his head fall into his hands. "I don't want to be like my father and brother who are so insensitive to everyone around them. I don't want to code all day or be pretentious at night in a room full of other pretentious people. I want to be somewhere quiet, and I want to write my stories."

"You're a walking cliché, Ravi Kumar," Jessie said, her voice light. She brushed at an errant curl at his temple.

He curled his lips slowly. "Just another rich, privileged South Asian kid who doesn't realize what he's got, right? God, I sound like a fucking sad-little-rich-boy pity party, Jessie. I hate it. I hate myself for it, but I don't know what I'm supposed to do."

Because she felt like he could use the comfort instead of a pep talk, Jessie moved on instinct and ran her fingers through his hair until she cupped the back of his neck. She'd never done anything like it before and was surprised it felt so natural. More importantly, she felt the muscles in his neck relax at her touch. He leaned back against her fingers and closed his eyes.

"You're going to have to tell them," she said softly. "Otherwise, you'll just stay the sad little rich boy."

"Or I can pick the easiest internship I can find and just suck it up."

"Taking the spot away from someone who worked really hard for that job because they really wanted it," she countered.

"Or taking the spot from some other VP's kid who's also getting special treatment. I'm sorry, Jessie, but there is rarely any fairness in my family's world. Are you sure it's one you want to potentially belong to someday?"

"Yes," she said with newfound conviction. "Yes, because I'll figure out a way to change the system. Or at least the parts of the system that I work within. Because I see it as an opportunity, a chance to have a career that my family always dreamed about but sacrificed for me. And that makes me *happy*, that I can fulfill their dreams. But if it doesn't make you happy, then don't do it."

He turned his head toward her, his eyes opening slowly. They were a warm, molten brown. "Do you think I'm pathetic?" he said softly.

"Pathetic because you want to be a writer instead of an engineer? No. Pathetic because your biggest problem in life is standing up to your parents? Maybe. But that's only because you have money and you don't lose out on anything other than relationships that already make you sad, Ravi."

"I guess you're right," he said. He closed his laptop and shifted it to the side. "I am being pathetic. So what do you think? Marketing or sales?"

Because she knew he was looking for a laugh, she pushed the blanket aside and moved to straddle his hips. "Marketing for sure. I don't think I could be with a sales guy."

His smile was infectious. He cupped her face in his hands and pressed a kiss against her lips. "Do I really have to pick one?" he asked softly.

"What would you do if you didn't work for your parents?"

"Write," he said immediately. "I don't know, maybe teach? The idea of grad school doesn't scare me, to be honest. I like school. And I mean that. Not the parties but the classes, too."

Jessie ran her hands over his chest, feeling the softness of his T-shirt and remembering the hardness underneath. "You know what you have to do."

He didn't answer her, instead leaning in for another kiss. "I wrote something else tonight. Do you want to know what it is?"

She could feel his arousal against the thin fabric of her panties. "Later," she whispered, and rocked against him, growing wetter with each tilt of her hips.

"Now," he said, and after groaning against her mouth, slipping his tongue between her lips, and digging his fingertips into her round butt cheeks for just a minute, holding her to him, he shifted her off to the side and back onto the couch.

"Ravi!"

"Just a minute," he said. Ravi picked up a folded piece of paper next to the tray on the coffee table. "Can you read this first?"

"It better be good," she mumbled. The uncomfortable heat of her arousal was a distraction, but she took the paper and unfolded it. Inside was his neatly printed handwriting. She pressed a hand to her chest. Delight shimmered in her veins. "You wrote me a letter?"

He nodded. "Read it."

She took a few deep breaths to manage the rush of emotion, of joy for this kind and beautiful man, before she started at the top of the page. "Dear Jaan . . ." She looked up at Ravi. "What—"

"Keep reading," he said quietly.

She cleared her throat. "'Dear Jaan, I chose this university because it was just acceptable enough for my family but no one before me had a legacy. I planned to create my own way and to make a name for myself in the four years I studied here. But then I met you, and my time here began to mean so much more. The moment we ran into each other, I felt like everything changed. I know you're worried about whether or not we belong together, and I won't lie to you, I'm worried, too. Not because I think that we don't, but because other people are going to try to stand in our way, and I don't know what I have to do to convince you that they are wrong. I love you more than I've loved anyone else in my life, and I know that if you give me a chance, I'll do my best to always put you first.'"

There were a few more lines left of the letter, but she couldn't read them. She couldn't see through her tears. Her heart was so full in that moment that she felt like it was about to burst from her chest. A soft sob escaped her mouth. "Ravi," she whispered.

"I love you," he said. He'd shifted so that he was crouched in front of her. He brushed a tear off her cheek with his thumb. "I love you, and no matter what else happens, that won't change."

But is it enough?

She couldn't voice the concern aloud, not when Ravi had just bared his heart to her.

"I love you, too," she said. Then she put the letter down on the coffee table. She wrapped her arms around his strong, warm frame, and she buried her face in the crook of his neck. "I love you, too."

Even if we break.

DECEMBER 15, 1971

Dear Jaan,

I'm sorry I ran yesterday. The force of your words scared me so much because I feel the same way. I love you, Christian. I love you more than I thought I'd ever love anyone in my life. But is love enough?

TWENTY-TWO

Jessie

RAVI: What are you doing next weekend again?

JESSIE: For Thanksgiving break? Nothing. I can't go back to Texas, so I'm probably going to have dinner with Tanvi's parents while you're with your folks.

RAVI: About that. They want to meet you.

JESSIE: Um . . . I thought you weren't going to tell them about us yet?

RAVI: I didn't. Sahdna said something because our parents are pressuring us to date again. Besides, she and Tanvi are spending Thanksgiving together.

JESSIE: Ravi, I don't know if that's the best idea.

RAVI: You're the only future engineer I know who isn't interested in meeting the Kumar family.

JESSIE: It's a commitment I don't think either of us are ready for yet. I mean we JUST started seeing each other.

RAVI: We started seeing each other the first day of the semester. Besides. It's the twenty-first century. I promise my parents won't read too much into it.

JESSIE: Bullshit. We aren't like our friends without color. Our culture is different.

RAVI: What's wrong with wanting my parents to meet my girlfriend, Jessie?

RAVI: You're important to me. I really want you to be there. Please?

JESSIE: Ugh. Fine. But not on Thanksgiving. Maybe that Wednesday before we all leave for the holiday. Okay?

RAVI: That's perfect. Thank you. I know I'm asking a lot.

Jessie wasn't able to sleep a full night for the few days leading up to the dinner with Ravi's parents. Every horrible outcome played through her head like a bad movie. What if they thought she was some gold digger and hated her so much they convinced the dean to cancel her scholarship? What if they threatened her father's business if she didn't leave their son alone? No, what if they hated her so much that Ravi saw the truth about how both of them were so ill-suited for each other?

"You look incredible," Tanvi said. She sat on her bed, cross-legged, with an open suitcase sitting in front of her. "I'm so glad you found that black dress."

Jessie let out a deep breath as she looked at her reflection in the small rectangular mirror that hung over her standard-issue armoire door. She'd bought the dress from the Macy's sales rack and had barely examined her reflection in the dressing room before she was out the door.

But now she saw how the slim black dress hugged her curves from neck to calves. Tanvi had let her borrow a small black clutch along with a pair of black boots that were both fashionable and practical for the weather.

She wore her mother's hoops. She rarely had an opportunity to put them on, but they were a gift from her grandmother to her mother on her wedding day.

And for the first time in her life, she had styled her hair into curls that fell down her back. That was also thanks to Tanvi's help. Her roommate had called it a late Diwali gift since Jessie's relationship with Ravi had introduced her to Sahdna. She'd even agreed to stay on campus for an extra night before driving home for the holidays just in case Jessie needed help getting ready.

Jessie felt her phone vibrate in her clutch and turned to her roommate. "I should head downstairs," she said. "I wouldn't be prepared for this without you. Thank you for all of your help. I don't have a lot of people in my life, because I know I can be a little uh, focused on work, but that just means the friends I do have are so important to me. I'll never forget this."

She winced as Tanvi's eyes began to water. She hadn't planned on making her roommate cry, and now she was worried that this was going to be a regular occurrence between them. Tanvi didn't seem to care that she was backing away and got off the bed and opened her arms for a hug. "Be careful with your heart," she whispered in Jessie's ear. "Please be careful."

"I will," Jessie said, even though she had a feeling that it might be too late when it came to her feelings about Ravi.

With one last look at her reflection in the mirror, Jessie left her room and rushed down the stairs to meet Ravi. When she pushed through the building's front doors, she saw him leaning against the back of a black sedan. The windows were tinted, and the rims were a shiny chrome. It was fitting for the way he looked under the streetlight: a fitted suit with an open white shirt, French cuffs with cuff links, pressed trousers, and black leather sneakers.

"Hi," she said, coming to a stop three feet from him.

"Wow," he said, his eyes widening. "Hi. You look incredible."

She swayed side to side, enjoying the feel of the dress hugging her skin. "Thanks, but don't get used to it. I'll be back in a sweatshirt and jeans in no time."

"You look great in those things, too."

She didn't wear a coat or even a shawl, and the exposed skin above the wide boat neck of her dress began to goose pimple from the chilly November air. "Any chance we can get going?"

He jumped into action and rounded the car so he could open the door for her. Like the princess she felt like she could never be, Jessie approached the car, then on a whim, she stood on her toes and pressed a soft kiss to the underside of his jaw.

"Thank you for finding me in that study room," she whispered.

"If you trust me, then I'll show you how awesome things can be outside of that study room, too."

As long as you stay with me.

This unspoken thought hung in the air between them as she slid across the buttery leather of the back seat until she was leaning against the opposite door. Ravi took his time getting back in the vehicle and shut the door with a quick thud. They were encased in darkness as the driver pulled away from the curb and onto the road.

"So," she said as they cruised down Main Street, "what's with the fancy vehicle? Why couldn't we drive or take a car service?"

His beautiful face was illuminated by brief flashes of streetlights. He turned to face her, his hand outstretched as if he couldn't stop himself from wanting to touch her to make sure she was still there. "The restaurant doesn't really have great parking, and I feel like my parents would spend the first fifteen minutes of our dinner talking about how unsafe it is to get into some stranger's car."

"Don't they own a ride-share company? I thought I read something in *Forbes*."

"My brother does," Ravi said. Jessie saw the slow movement of his throat.

"And even then, your family worries?"

"Yeah, I guess so."

The fact that his parents worried about his safety felt so . . . normal. But she knew this was an illusion. She remembered the way he'd told her how often he was alone growing up. How they rarely cared what he wanted and what he said was best for him.

"Hey, what did you tell your parents about me?"

Ravi squeezed her hand. "I just said that you were probably the most surprising thing that I've ever had in my life and I'm grateful that you're a part of it now."

She felt her heart melt just a little bit and had to work at reinforcing the ice that she'd encased around her feelings. "Didn't they ask about what I was studying? What my parents did for a living? If it's going to be like an interview, then I'm screwed."

Ravi swallowed. "They did, and I answered honestly. They're very impressed, by the way. And no, they'll probably do most of the talking."

Great, she thought. At least that was something. But she knew that her interest in engineering would also highlight the fact that Ravi hadn't picked an internship yet.

The car pulled up a few minutes later in front of an Italian restaurant at the edge of town. As cliché as it was, Jessie assumed they'd be going to an Indian restaurant. But maybe they were looking for something different.

Ravi opened the door, pulling her out of her thoughts. He helped her slide out from the back seat and get her bearings on the sidewalk before he shut the door and tucked one of her hands under his arm.

"Are you ready?" he asked.

No. "Yes."

"Great," he said, and sucked in a deep breath. She did the same as they strolled into the restaurant and toward the private room at the back that was monitored by two large men in suits flanking the door. They had to be security.

The first person she saw was Neeraj Kumar. The man who had periodically made an appearance on her parents' television stood from his seat at the end of the table. The handsome features of his youth had become more rugged and distinguished with age. He didn't bother crossing the room or hugging his son. Instead, he greeted them in a booming voice.

"Ravi."

The next person to stand was one of the most beautiful women Jessie had ever seen. Ravi's mother was a vision in a sleek column dress and diamond stud earrings. Unlike Ravi's father, she rounded the table and crossed the room so she could wrap her son in a hug that showed she didn't give two damns about the way she looked if she could hold her child.

The last people to get up from the table were Ravi's older brother and a woman who, Jessie learned just that morning when she was doing a Google search, was his girlfriend.

"Papa, Mumma," Ravi said, an arm still around his mother's waist. "I want you to meet Jessie Ahuja."

Jessie braced herself for a cold front, a frigid smile dripping with ice. Instead, she found herself enveloped in the same hug Ravi had just received. She caught the delicate scent of jasmine flowers before she took a step back and clasped her hands in front of her.

"Jessie," Ravi's father said in that same booming voice. He nodded.

"Thank you so much for inviting me to dinner tonight. I really appreciate it."

"We're really curious about you, so it's our pleasure," Ravi's older brother said.

Jessie approached the table and accepted the handshakes from Arjun Kumar and his girlfriend before sitting down between Ravi and Ravi's mother.

They ordered wine because Ravi had been drinking it since he was eighteen, at least in front of his parents. Then they asked the chef to deliver what he thought was best. Jessie's chest tightened as she watched everyone's focus shift to her.

"So," Ravi's father said. "Jessie, Ravi tells me you just started at the university and you're in his nonfiction writing class."

"Ah, yes," she said, even though she could feel Ravi tense by her side.

"And you're in the engineering school?" Arjun asked. "Software or hardware?"

"I'm not sure yet, so I front-loaded my gen-ed courses. I'm hoping to get a better idea based on the internships I can get over the summer."

She winced the minute she said the word *internship*. Jessie tried to reach under the table to touch Ravi's knee, but he was too far away from her. She saw how his jaw had tightened.

"Well, at least one of you has common sense," Arjun said before he sipped at the glass of table water.

Jessie had to bite her lip to stop from telling him to shove his sarcasm up his ass.

"Oh, don't start pestering him so soon," Ravi's mother said. "Right now, I want to get to know Jessie."

"Your father owns a sandwich shop, Jessie?" Ravi's father asked.

She could see Ravi tense again. At this rate, his spine was going to crack.

Jessie turned to the man she had always considered larger than life. It was so surreal sitting so close to him, seeing him as her boyfriend's father instead of just another tech genius to walk the planet.

"Yes, my father owns a franchise location," Jessie said. "It's in Houston. Both of my parents were engineers before the market crashed and they lost their jobs. For employment safety, they ended up pivoting into food services. They've been doing pretty well for themselves, and they're happy."

There was that awkward silence that she had anticipated. The one that told her that Ravi's parents didn't think her background was good enough for her to be dating their son.

"They must be really proud of you for getting a full scholarship," Arjun's girlfriend said. She wore an elegant blue dress, her hair parted down the middle and pulled back in a tight bun. She looked like the perfect partner, a daughter-in-law in the making.

"My parents *are* really proud of me," Jessie said as the waiter presented the bottle of wine to Ravi's father. "They know that even though I have no intention of taking over the family business, they taught me everything I know to succeed after I graduate."

Ravi's father lifted his glass, smelled the wine, then swirled it while making a show of examining the coloring. He nodded, and the waiter began filling everyone's glass.

There was more silence. Someone coughed. Ravi shifted in the seat next to Jessie as if he wasn't sure what to say. She wanted to snap at him, to tell him that this is what she had warned him about.

"So when did you two start dating?" Ravi's father asked.

"A few months ago," Ravi said.

"Jessie, are you the reason why my brother hasn't chosen an internship?" Arjun asked with a laugh.

"Ravi knows how important the decision is to all of you. I think your pushing and interference is probably the reason why he hasn't chosen an internship, not me."

Her words landed like a bull's-eye hitting its target.

They hadn't even ordered dinner yet, and things were already uncomfortable. Jessie was regretting her decision to come at all. Even though Ravi had invited her, she should have stuck to her gut and skipped out on the Kumar family affair.

"I guess you're just going to parties all the time, then," Neeraj Kumar said, his frown deepening. "It's a good thing that I had that conversation with the dean at USC, because it looks like you may be transferring for your last year after all."

Jessie could feel the tension flooding Ravi's body, the tightening of his muscles, even though they were sitting nearly a foot apart. She wanted to reach out and comfort him, but she felt like if she did, they'd only blame him more for being distracted.

"I had midterms," Ravi said, his jaw so tense that Jessie swore she could hear his teeth grind. "And I'm working on a personal project."

His mother brightened, as if waiting for the opportunity to throw a lifeline to her son in these shark-infested waters. "Is it an app? Or are you working on a coding project? You always were so quick to learn new coding languages with your father," she said. "Tell us, beta. We want the opportunity to support you."

"Yeah, tell us," Arjun said, his voice laced with sarcasm.

"I'm working on a novel, actually."

Their response was almost instantaneous. Jessie watched as both Arjun and Neeraj Kumar leaned back in their chairs and began to laugh. The sound was more cutting and hurtful than any words could have been.

"AI is going to make the entertainment industry obsolete," Arjun said. "Why would you waste your time with something like that? Dad was right. All those trashy books have rotted your brain."

"We're making this so easy for you," Neeraj said. "All you have to do is choose! It's like you're intentionally trying to be stubborn about it," he snapped.

"Well, prepare to be even more disappointed, then," Ravi said quietly. "Because I'm going to stay on campus this summer instead of working at either of your companies. I want to take some extra classes because I think I want to apply for a grad program in English."

If Jessie thought the table was silent before, she was pretty sure she'd now be able to hear a pin drop from down the block.

"What in the world do you need a graduate degree for?" Neeraj finally said. "In *English*? A field with zero financial stability? We're giving you more than most people could even dream of! My son, the only one in our whole family to waste such an opportunity."

Jessie couldn't hold back any longer. She shifted her chair closer to Ravi, and reached under the table and rested her palm against his thigh. Everyone around the table watched her with shocked expressions. That probably made them dislike her even more.

"I don't see it as an opportunity. I'm as passionate about this as you are about tech. You know I've always been a reader."

"That's true," Ravi's mother said faintly. "You've always had a book in your hand."

"So I should blame *you* for this?" Neeraj Kumar said, his voice hardening as he turned to his wife. "For coddling him like he's a baby?"

"Neeraj—"

How many times had this family been in a standoff similar to this where both brothers went head-to-head? Where Ravi's father acted like the Indian father that Jessie was lucky to only hear stories about?

"Jessie," the older man finally said, turning his wrath on her. "What do you think of Ravi's plans of going to graduate school?"

She couldn't lie to him. "If my family had the money and the stability and legacy that yours has, then my parents would want me to do whatever I wanted to do with my life. If that meant going to grad school, they would give me their blessing. I mean, why else would you want to be so successful and financially independent if not to support those you love?"

The man nodded. "Your parents don't have money and stability and legacy. They own a sandwich shop, which means that they'll never understand what it's like to be in our position."

"That's exactly my point—"

"My family runs companies," he continued. "We know that the way we've gotten to where we are is by making sacrifices and choosing the career path that will ensure our financial success."

"Your oldest son seems to have sacrificed for the next generation. When is it enough?"

"When both my sons are successful and stable and secure," Neeraj Kumar said, his voice raising with each word. "A decision that I made, and you don't have the right to question."

"Well, someone has to," Jessie said. Her ears were ringing, her breath coming fast. "Or is that how you run your company? By demanding respect instead of earning it?"

The room was even quieter now than when she first walked in, and she knew that she'd destroyed any chance she had at all of playing nice with the Kumars.

"I see that your upbringing failed you in the manners department as well. I wonder, is your influence the reason why my son has made so many poor decisions?"

Jessie shot to her feet before she could think twice about it. She looked down at Ravi's face and knew.

"I'm so sorry, I have to go," she said to the man she'd fallen in love with. "Thank you so much for inviting me."

She reached down to grab her purse, then ran through the restaurant until she reached the parking lot. She didn't know exactly where she wanted to go, but anywhere would be better than here.

When she saw Sahdna walking toward the entrance, panic bubbled in her throat. She was wearing five-inch heels and a white dress that hugged her like a second skin. Sahdna's eyes widened when she caught sight of Jessie.

"Jessie? What are you doing here? What's wrong?"

Jessie stopped inches away from her. She looked over her shoulder and saw that no one had come out after her yet. "I was invited to have dinner with Ravi's parents."

She gasped. "You, too?"

The sickening truth slapped her in the face. "Of course," Jessie said, motioning to Sahdna. "They probably invited you to make Ravi realize he's dating the wrong girl."

She shook her head, her gorgeous waves floating over her shoulders and down her back. "Ravi and I are old news. But our families are still friends. I'm just doing this because my parents would kill me if I didn't play nice." She looked past Jessie to the door of the restaurant. "I'm so sorry."

"Don't be," Jessie said. She couldn't hide her bitterness. "It was the reality check I needed." Even if Ravi loved her, there was absolutely no way he would go against his parents in the end. Because the truth was, he wasn't just fighting a battle with the two people who raised him. He was fighting the entire legacy his family had built within the Indian community. The Kumar tech conglomerate meant success for South Asians, and even though the notion that anyone could achieve what his parents had was somewhat false, it still offered hope. Jessie was living proof of that hope, whether she liked to admit it or not.

Sahdna looked back at the door, and to Jessie again. "What are you gonna do now?"

Jessie motioned to the road. "I'm just going to walk a block and call a car so no one can see me from the restaurant."

"No way," Sahdna said. "Ravi would have my head if he found out I let you go without someone driving you home." She opened her sleek white clutch and pulled out a small key fob. "Come on. Campus isn't too far from here. I'll take you home, and then I can swing back. It'll give them time to cool off."

Jessie nodded. Sahdna had obligations. She had her own demons to wrestle with. Of course she was going to come back.

"Just because I don't know if Ravi is going to come after me, I'll take that ride."

She nodded. "Good. Come on. I parked at the end of the lot."

With one last look at the restaurant door, Jessie followed Sahdna across the lot to the white Tesla Model Y. The interior revealed that Sahdna was as much of a clean freak as Ravi. Another thing they had in common.

A few seconds later, they were pulling out of the lot and back onto the highway that led to the campus.

"I'm sorry they put you in that position," Sahdna said quietly. "They can be really tough. But don't take it personally. They judge everyone. My parents are the same. I think it comes with the territory. They treat their families like their employees."

Jessie twisted her fingers in her lap, unsure of what to say in response.

Sahdna flipped on her turn signal and merged right. "He cares about you, you know. He would have never brought you here if he didn't think that you were important to him."

"I'm sure I am. But we all know that being at college is like living inside a bubble. What's going to happen when we leave? His parents sure seem to know this, and Ravi, no matter what he feels about me, is going to end up with someone his parents approve of." Jessie looked over at Sahdna meaningfully.

Sahdna merged onto the exit ramp and pulled to a stop at the light. She turned in her seat, her brown hair shimmering in the passing headlights. "I'm going to be straight with you, Jessie. I also don't think you deserve Ravi."

Jessie felt like she'd stopped breathing.

"Ravi deserves to be with someone who isn't so caught up in their own insecurities. You're so focused on the fact that you come from different worlds, that you don't have as much money as him, that you're driving a wedge between yourselves. From everything I know about you, you've done nothing but make him nervous that you're going to leave him any minute. Then the first shitty family dinner, you get up and run away. That's your right, but that doesn't mean Ravi deserves to have to put up with someone who doesn't support him the same way he's been supporting them."

"That's easy for you to say when you don't understand what it's like to be in my position."

"That's true," Sahdna replied. "But I know Ravi, and he needs someone he can trust will look past where he's come from. So no, I don't think that you deserve Ravi. I just hope you're not cruel and that you'll have the decency to put him out of his misery."

At that moment, the light changed, and Sahdna pressed her foot against the gas. Jessie felt the sick nausea in her gut that had started at dinner crawl into her throat.

Sahdna was right, she thought. She was the one who was driving a wedge between them with her constant concerns about how different they were.

She couldn't help but think about Divya and Christian. Ever since they had talked to Gayatri and Professor Barnard, Jessie worried that maybe the true love they found on campus wasn't enough to keep them together. She had to find out what happened to them.

That meant one thing. Jessie was going to break her promise to Ravi and read the rest of the letters on her own.

MAY 19, 1972

Dear Jaan,

This may be the last letter I ever write to you.

TWENTY-THREE

Ravi

W hat was the point in inviting her to dinner?" Ravi shouted. "To embarrass her in front of everyone?" He had to know before he went after Jessie.

"You actually think this is about *her*?" Arjun asked. "Dude, this is about you, and your ridiculous plans to get a graduate degree in *English*."

Ravi looked at his brother, fisting his hands at his sides. "You're so desperate to be just like Dad, Arjun. How's that going for you? Last article I read, your start-up was having a hard time getting funding because it lacked originality."

Arjun rushed to his feet. "Fuck you, Ravi. At least I'm doing something meaningful with my life."

Ravi stood to face him, hands flat on the table. "Is that what you want to call it?"

"Sit down," Ravi's father snapped. He motioned to the empty, private room. "You're making a scene in public."

"I'm going after Jessie," Ravi said. He leaned across the table so that he faced his parents. "Dada came to this country so that he could make a better life for our family. He did what he had to do so that we could all be successful. He would've *wanted* us to have a choice. Because that's what he fought for."

"You're right," his father said, his voice razor-sharp. "Your dada made sacrifices, and it's time you learn that you have to make sacrifices, too. Do you think we're asking you to consider an internship because of *us*? No, this is about what's best for *you*, Ravi. Because what are you going to do in twenty years with your English degree? With your little writing projects? You'll have no one and nothing."

The words cut across his soul, and he felt himself sinking back in his seat, making himself small, the way he used to when he was young.

"Can we please stop talking about this for now?" Ravi's mother pleaded. "Ravi, we're so sorry that your girlfriend is upset, but we came all this way to see you. The least you can do is just finish the meal with us. I promise we won't mention the internship again. Just stay."

He could hear the tension, the panic in her voice, and he hated that she was always trying so desperately to be the peacemaker. He could see the same panic on Arjun's girlfriend's face. She would become the same kind of peacemaker that his mother had become.

Just as he was about to text Jessie to ask if she was okay, his phone buzzed with an incoming text.

SAHDNA: I ran into Jessie in the parking lot. I'm going to drive her back to her dorm before I join you for dinner. I thought you knew, but your parents invited me. I'm going to be there out of obligation, but if you can think of an excuse, I'm happy to bow out.

All thoughts of staying, of trying to repair the fissures in his relationship with his family, disintegrated. "Did you invite Sahdna?" he asked, cutting his mother off from her nervous rambling about a family friend's upcoming wedding.

"We haven't seen her in a long time," his mother said. "We thought it would be a good idea to see her—"

"At the same time that I was bringing my girlfriend to meet you?" he asked.

"Watch your tone," his father snapped. Then he switched to Hindi, which he rarely spoke anymore. "That's your mother you're talking to."

"Did you learn that little parenting line from your all-White executive leadership board? Did they also teach you how to ignore your family?"

"Ravi!" the table shouted at him unanimously.

Maybe some relationships were bound to fail from the beginning, Ravi thought. He had to start focusing on the people that he knew would accept him for who he was and who he wanted to become.

He stood from the table. "Thanks for coming to Jersey," he said quietly. "Happy Diwali and Happy Thanksgiving." Then he walked out of the restaurant to look for his girlfriend.

Ravi took a deep breath and knocked. There was a pause, a sniffle, and then the sound of bedsprings squeaking before the door opened a crack.

Jessie's bloodshot eyes widened, then she pulled open the door all the way. It was the first time he'd been to her dorm room. He'd managed to get into the freshman towers because someone had held open the door when they recognized who he was.

There were two single beds on opposite sides of the room. Tanvi's side was purple and pink, with posters and string lights, while Jessie's was decorated simply, with a plain floral bedspread, books stacked on her bedside table, and a desk at the foot of her bed. He looked down at her, standing at the entrance to her room.

"What are you doing here? Your parents. Dinner . . ."

"Baby, I'm so sorry," he said hoarsely.

He stepped inside the room, then froze. His heart took a dive to his stomach. Strewn across her bed, in no particular order, were all of Divya Das's letters.

All of them. Including the ten that they were supposed to open the following week. Jessie had gone ahead and read everything on her own instead of waiting for him to share the moment. Not that he could blame her. He should've followed her out of the restaurant, but he'd stayed, even if only for a brief amount of time. It was probably enough to convince her that he wasn't serious about their relationship. Ravi cleared his throat, then turned to her. He saw the guilt written across her face.

"What did they say?"

"What?"

"What do the letters say?" He crossed the small room to her bed and picked up one of the pages before waving it gently like a fan. "Did you find anything else in here that would lead us to believe that they're still together somewhere, living their happily ever after?"

Please be together. I need something to believe in.

Jessie's eyes welled with tears. "Y-yes, I know what happened."

"Well?" he said, his heart breaking all over again. "What do the letters say?" He didn't mean to raise his voice, but he couldn't help it. He couldn't stop.

"Ravi . . . they broke up."

Of all the things he expected her to tell him, that was not it. In theory, he knew that was a possibility for Divya and Christian. Reality was a cruel bitch sometimes, and people had tragic lives. But somewhere along the way, he'd started to hope for a different kind of ending. He stumbled back and hit the side of her bed frame. "W-what?"

Jessie nodded. "I read the last letter. She broke up with him. She said that she wasn't going to be responsible for his sadness. For how much he'd resent her for leaving his family. And she said that she planned on going through with the arranged marriage in India. She wished him well."

"No," Ravi said. He'd started shaking his head before she even finished. "No, I don't believe it. I can't believe it. They fought so hard to keep their relationship a secret, they fell so deeply in love that both of us fell, too—"

"Don't say that," she rushed. Her tears fell freely now. "Don't even think it."

He reached for her, but she stumbled back. "I can't," he said, feeling the tears well in his own eyes. "I can't not think about how much I love you and how much I would give up to be with you, too."

Jessie pressed a letter against her chest so hard that the paper began to crease. "Divya is right, Ravi. Life is not all hearts and candy. It's not about love notes in beautiful libraries. Sometimes life is about responsibility to those who helped us get where we are. It's about putting our families before ourselves. We're going to be totally fine. I mean, we are so privileged, you and I. We'll get through the rest of the semester then stay clear of each other. This is just a blip in our lives and we'll move on and remember each other like any other relationship. But we will be better if we aren't together."

He couldn't breathe. "You don't mean that."

"I can't explain their disappearance," Jessie continued as she wiped her nose on the back of her pajama sleeves. "But if I were to guess, I'd say both of them pulled out of school that day, and people decided they'd prefer to imagine they ran off together. But that love story isn't real and, Ravi, neither is ours."

He stepped forward, wrapped his arms around her waist, and crashed his lips down onto hers. He was unyielding, taking everything he could from her the same way she'd robbed him of happiness. Maybe one day he'd realize that he could move on and he'd find happiness with someone else, but right now, and in his heart, he knew he'd never be the same. So he'd take this kiss, the soft give of her mouth. He'd remember the pressure of her hands as she fisted the back of his shirt and how she tried to get impossibly closer to his body. He'd remember her love and the understanding in her eyes and the way her laugh sounded in the dark.

When the pain was too much, he pulled away. They were both gasping for air, tears pouring down their cheeks. They cried for the love that ended fifty years ago and for the love that they were giving up right now, so young and sudden.

"It'll be hard to see you on campus," she said quietly, "but it's better this way."

"I have to go," Ravi said as he wiped his tears. "I love you and probably always will, but right now, I have to go." He took the letter that was crumpled in her hands, pressed one final kiss against the corner of her mouth, then left.

TWENTY-FOUR

Ravi

Ravi hadn't vaped in so long that the first pull on his pen left him dizzy and nauseous. But his body soon remembered the sweet, addictive taste, and he quickly worked through the first small cartridge he'd purchased that night.

He rarely spent Saturdays alone at home. In the three years he'd been on campus, he could probably count on one hand the times his weekend nights involved sitting on his balcony, smoking. But here he was, looking down at the traffic on the street below his condo building, hearing the soft hum of the TV he'd left on behind the glass doors.

Ravi wasn't ashamed that he'd come back to his condo, stripped out of all of his clothes, and then cried in the shower for his broken heart and his broken love. He felt like he was being ripped to shreds, when in reality, they hadn't been together long at all. One semester. No, half of a semester. The first half was just them circling each other. Then their differences became enough to separate them for good.

He took another slow pull from the pen, then let out a stream of smoke that unfurled into the dark night. It had all happened so fast, but it felt like a lifetime. He knew her quirks, her likes, her dislikes, her habits. He understood her hopes and dreams, and he'd shared his own, which he'd never done with anyone before. And that was an intimacy that was so rare for him to have with anyone that it was inevitable he'd start to fall in love with her.

The letter sat beside him, tucked under a crystal whiskey glass filled two-thirds of the way with dark-amber liquid. Just as he was about to take a sip, there was a sharp knock on the door inside.

Who the hell was coming over at midnight?

He crossed the room and looked into the peephole before cursing.

"I know you're in there," Arjun called out. "I heard you swearing."

"These fucking doors suck," he said, then unlatched the chain to let in his brother, wearing a rumpled suit and bags under his eyes. "What are you doing here, bhai? How did you even know where I live?"

Arjun shrugged. "I assumed you're drinking whiskey alone, so I figured I'd come and join you. And we all know where you live. You're dumb enough to send Diwali presents to us from this address."

Shit.

"You've known all this time? And you want to now join me for whiskey?" Ravi was taken aback by this unexpected proposal. As adults, he and his brother had never spent time alone together. While they had relied on each other's company as kids, in the last few years, it had always been Ravi pitted against his father and brother.

Arjun nodded as if this were a completely normal occurrence. "Dad is shit company lately, so I'm choosing the lesser of the two."

"Considering Jessie and I just broke up, you may have chosen wrong."

"Ahh," Arjun said. He rocked back on his heels.

"Happy?" Ravi said ruefully. "I bet that's what you wanted."

In a surprising move, Arjun clasped Ravi's shoulder. "I'm sorry. But it's better that it happens now than later."

Ravi turned toward the liquor cart and picked up a half-empty bottle. "How does it feel to be exactly what Mom and Dad always wanted?"

Arjun cocked his head as he slipped out of his suit coat. "I don't know, since Mom and Dad have always been critical of me, too."

"Bullshit," Ravi said bitterly.

Arjun took the glass that Ravi handed him. "Can I tell you something?"

"As my older brother, I feel like you're going to regardless of what I say."

Arjun shrugged. "You're not wrong. Come on. Let's go sit outside."

Ravi didn't feel like he had a choice, so he led his brother into the cold November air. Arjun took a seat and picked up one of the vape pens.

"Do you mind?" he asked.

"I guess not."

Arjun settled in, took half of Ravi's blanket, and as if it were a totally normal occurrence, he vaped and drank in silence next to Ravi's side.

"I guess I didn't have any idea how lucky I was. I knew that I wanted to be a part of the family business since I was a kid," he finally said. "I heard what you said to Dad today, and I realized that if I was in your shoes, it would suck not having someone on my side."

"It does," Ravi said. He studied his brother's profile. "And I don't resent you for wanting to be like Dad. But I do resent Mom and Dad for not realizing that I'm different than you."

"And I've been pushing you, too."

Ravi gave him a rueful smile. "You've been an absolute dick."

There was another stretch of silence, leaving Ravi to wonder if his brother had always been so contemplative.

"If you want to go to grad school," Arjun said slowly, "then go to fucking grad school. Stay here as long as you want with Jessie. But you'll have to deal with the consequences and prove that it's worth the sacrifice."

A familiar itching sensation crept up the base of his spine, an uneasy discomfort that always resurfaced when discussing his future with his family. "Do you know why I chose media studies?"

Arjun rolled his eyes. "To piss off Dad?"

"No, that's never been my goal despite what you both think. It's because I get to tell stories. I get to analyze what tech companies do and craft a narrative about it. That was as close to a compromise as I could make. Be true to myself and also study something that may one day be applicable to the family business."

"Yeah, the marketing department might benefit from—"

"Arjun," Ravi said, cutting him off. "If there is one thing I've learned, it's that compromising isn't going to work. Dad is still going to be unhappy. You'll still be critical of everything I do. So if media studies doesn't make all of us happy with my role in supporting the family, I might as well say 'fuck it' and do what makes me happy and just deal with your disappointment. Because as Desi as we all are, I'm privileged enough to be able to walk away from the Kumar family if I want."

Arjun let out a deep breath and took a sip of his whiskey. "Okay."

Ravi stared at his brother. "Okay? What do you mean by 'okay'?"

"I mean, as long as you're willing to deal with the consequences. I'll *try* to support you. Even if I disagree. You may go down a few wrong paths, but hopefully you'll pick yourself up and move forward."

The words had an ominous tone to them, and then he realized what Arjun was trying to do. "Is this a fucking segue to my love life?"

"That it is," Arjun said cheerfully. "That it fucking is."

Ravi closed his eyes and rested his head on the back of his patio chair. "There's nothing to discuss. Like I said, Jessie broke up with me."

"Is there anything you can say or do to make her give you another chance? Flowers? Gifts? A singing telegram?"

"Wait, I thought you didn't like Jessie," Ravi said, sitting up in his chair.

Arjun shrugged. "Look, I'm not a great brother, and we both know that. But you're dating an engineer. If that's as close as you're getting to the family business, then I guess we'll have to take it."

For the first time in years, Ravi laughed without reservation. He still remembered the harsh words that they shared at dinner, the raw feelings they had about each other, but in this moment, their connection superseded all of that.

His thoughts circled back to Arjun's question about Jessie. "I don't know what I can do to convince her," he said. "She thinks that we come from these completely separate worlds, and in a way, she's not wrong. But she's so afraid of who we'll be after we graduate. I think it's because she sees me leaving college before her and going back West, leaving her behind."

"Is that why you're considering graduate school? So you can stay with her?"

"It's mostly for me," he said. But Ravi would be lying if he didn't admit the obvious perk of being able to stay with Jessie, too. They'd had such a short relationship over the course of one semester, but it was enough to solidify his feelings about her. "I think she sees our fate as being entwined with Christian and Divya's."

"*Who?*" Arjun asked.

Ravi laughed. He'd been so engrossed in the mystery that he hadn't realized there were people outside of Hartceller who had never heard of the legend. "Here's a problem that your code will never be able to solve," Ravi said.

He gave Arjun the rundown: the campus legend, where the letters were found, what they said, and their interviews with Gayatri and Professor Barnard. When he was done, their glasses were empty and the cartridge was almost finished. The wind had picked up, and it was freezing now.

"I think you should write Jessie a letter," Arjun said. "I think that's the best way you can get things across to her. Just like your Divya Das wrote letters to Christian."

"I already have. I poured my heart out, man. And I doubt another letter could fix things. I mean, look what happened with the last letter between Divya and Christian."

He picked up the folded envelope from under his glass and handed it to Arjun. In the dim overhead lighting of his balcony, Arjun took a few minutes to read the missive carefully. He brought it so close to his face that his nose practically touched the ink. He raised an eyebrow and gave a low whistle before laying it down.

"What did he say?"

Ravi tilted his head. "What did who say?"

"Christian. What did he say in response to her intention to break up?"

"I don't know. We only have Divya's letters."

"Did you look for Christian's?"

Ravi felt a tickling sensation in the back of his throat. "No," he said slowly. "We left the library as fast as we could. The tower is locked because they're starting renovations over winter break." Had he really never thought about Christian's side of the story?

"Do you think his letters might still be in there? In the desk?"

Ravi shrugged. Considering everything he knew about Divya Das and her lover, there should've been more letters. The more he thought about it, the more he knew that there had to be letters. Because if Christian loved Divya as much as she loved him, then he'd express the same feelings on paper in return.

Ravi bolted to his feet. "I have to write a letter to Jessie."

Arjun rolled his eyes. "My work here is done. Maybe I'm not that much of a shit brother after all."

"No, no, it's not," Ravi said. "I can't write this letter without showing her that there's another side to the story. I have to find Christian's letters first."

"How are you going to do that?" Arjun asked. "Didn't you just say that Davidson Tower is locked?"

"Yeah." He grinned at his brother. "Hey, want to go on an adventure? Like old times when we were kids and stuck at home with the nanny? Think of the weekend we camped out in the treehouse and made ourselves sick on Fritos and Capri Sun. You know. Before you became an absolute douche like Dad."

Arjun smiled, and for a moment, he looked like their mom. "For you? I guess we can do it like old times."

Ravi picked up his phone and called Deep. "Yo!" he said into the receiver over the sound of a rave. "We need those library keys again. In, like, five minutes."

It was ridiculously easy, breaking into Davidson Tower for a second time. With Deep's keys in hand and his brother by his side, Ravi entered the library through the back service entrance and walked straight down to the basement. They crossed the floor behind the stacks and waited to make sure that there was no patrol before walking up to the locked doors of Davidson Tower. How many times had he looked through his study room into the tower to see the kaleidoscope-like stained-glass ceiling? How many times had he wondered what it would be like to study inside the tower? More importantly, how many times had he pictured Jessie sitting at the table, smiling at him when he walked in?

After using one of the metal keys on Deep's key ring to unlock Davidson Tower, Ravi pulled open the wood door and stepped inside. Arjun was ominously quiet behind him, taking in the dusty surroundings.

"The desk was upstairs," Ravi said.

Arjun made a slow circle, taking in the room. "We definitely didn't have anything like this at MIT."

"You didn't have to come, you know."

Arjun looked back at Ravi. "Yeah, I probably did. I still want to see Dad's face when you and your girlfriend stand up to him again about grad school."

"Ahh, my dickhead brother is back."

"I never left," Arjun said with a chuckle. "But this time, I'll make a case for grad school on your behalf, too. If we survive this haunted-tower bullshit."

Ravi shook his head. He doubted Arjun's brief moment of empathy would stop him from acting like an asshole for the rest of his life, so he'd take advantage of his brother's help while he could.

They made their way to the back of the tower room, then ascended the spiral staircase to the second level. Armed with a flashlight they had brought, Ravi carefully removed the sheet covering the desk and proceeded to check every nook and cranny—examining the drawers, the back paneling, the underside of the desk, and inside all the cabinet spaces.

Twenty minutes later, they were still empty-handed.

"I feel like I'm missing something," Ravi said as he sat back on his haunches in front of the desk.

Arjun nodded, then scanned the row of boxes behind them. "What were the letters stored in? The ones from Divya."

"A book," Ravi said. "An old copy of a Jane Austen novel."

"Maybe there's another Jane Austen novel that Christian put his letters in. I would try to make it as obvious as possible. I'm a software engineer, so my brain would want to find parallels."

"Another Jane Austen novel," he mused. Then he remembered the box of books that Jessie was looking at before he interrupted her. He flashed his light in their direction. The box labeled 1972 was sitting right where Jessie had left it, with its flaps open.

"There," he said. He handed the flashlight to his brother, then picked up the box to put on the desk. On the very top was a mirror copy of Jane Austen's *Persuasion*. He'd been so busy trying to get Jessie out of the library the last time they were there that he hadn't thought to dig any further.

"Bingo," Arjun said.

Ravi held his breath as he lifted the cover. Inside, there was a hollowed-out section fitted with a stack of letters just as thick as those from Divya Das.

Just like the first time he'd seen the letters, he felt a spark of hope. Maybe, just maybe, he could repair what he'd started with Jessie.

"Come on, Christian," Ravi murmured. "Help me get my girl back."

TWENTY-FIVE

Jessie

Jessie felt utterly lost as she approached her last nonfiction class, not knowing how to begin writing her paper for Professor Barnard. She should have taken her professor's advice during their office hours. Now she was filled with panic and heartbreak. Panic because all the effort she had invested in finding the closure that she so desperately needed for Divya Das and herself was coming to an end with zero results.

It didn't help that she was aching, every part of her heart and her soul, because she missed being with Ravi, who understood her like no one else. She was operating on autopilot. In the four days she'd been on Thanksgiving break, she'd get up, shower, dress, have breakfast, study, go to work, and come home. Rinse and repeat. She called her parents every day; told them she was fine, even though they heard the heartbreak in her voice; and feigned exhaustion before she went to bed.

And sometimes, she'd cry. She hated crying. It was a waste of time and energy, but for Ravi? She cried in the shower, and when Tanvi wasn't in the room, she'd cry herself to sleep.

She couldn't wait to go home so she could lay her head in her mother's lap and hold her father's hand, because she knew that she'd then have some time to properly fall apart. In the meantime, she had to hold it together until her classes were over.

Just as she was about to enter the building that housed her lecture hall, her phone buzzed in her pocket. She answered, smiling for the first time since Saturday night.

"Hi, Daddy."

"Hello, my munchkin," he said warmly. "We missed you so much for Thanksgiving. Did you have fun?"

Jessie stepped to the side so other people could enter the building behind her. "I had a great time," she lied. "The next time you come, we should all go out to dinner."

"Absolutely," he said with a chuckle. "And how is Ravi doing? I know his family was in town."

"Actually, Daddy—" She paused, realizing what he had just said. "Wait a minute, how do you know his family was in town?"

Her father chuckled again. "That's why I wanted to call you. I got a call from Ravi's brother, Arjun. He rang me at the store, and he asked if I was interested in going back to consulting. His company has something called an upskill program where they educate people who are in their forties and fifties on the latest technology so they can reenter the workforce. Your mom and I are considering it. I still have twenty-five years left before I retire and I don't know if I want to spend it in retail. Tell Ravi we appreciate that he put in a good word for us. It means a lot."

Jessie's mind raced with the news. She was so sure that Ravi's father and brother hated her. What was going on?

"Daddy, I thought you loved the business."

"We do! And we love our store. We may keep it but just have someone else run it, which means that we won't make much money, but we'll be happier. We can talk about that later. I know you have a class coming up."

"Right," she said. "Daddy, what are you going to do when you don't have a picture of all of the classes that I registered for next semester?"

She heard the soft sadness in his voice before he spoke. "I'll miss my daughter, and I'll wait for her to call me back."

Damn it, she thought. She was going to end up giving him a copy of her schedule after all. That was after she talked to Ravi to find out what the hell was happening.

She checked her watch. "Daddy? I love you."

"Be good in class! I love you, too," he said before hanging up.

Jessie hated that class was about to start because she wanted to talk to Ravi. He needed to respect her boundaries. Going behind her back to try to help her parents was so low, so underhanded, so . . . effective. The more he involved himself in her life, the harder it would be to say goodbye. The more she'd feel indebted to him. Didn't he realize that she couldn't give him the same opportunities that he was giving to her and her family?

She yanked open the door to the building where they had class and practically jogged all the way to the lecture hall. When she entered, Professor Barnard still hadn't arrived.

But Ravi was there.

He stood behind her row, backpack slung over one shoulder and a white envelope in one hand. Knowing that people were watching her, she evened her stride so that she didn't look like she was running toward him, which was exactly what she wanted to do, and slid into her row.

"What are you doing, Ravi?" she asked, her voice low.

"Waiting for you," he said. He handed her the white envelope. "Here. I think you should read this."

She should refuse it, but since people were still watching them, she took the envelope. Before she could turn around and take her seat, Ravi cupped her cheek, then leaned down to kiss the corner of her mouth.

The touch sparked heat and fire low in her belly, coursing through her skin like it had ever since the first time they'd kissed. Then he was gone, and she was collapsing into her seat.

Since Professor Barnard still hadn't arrived yet, she looked over her shoulder where Ravi had chosen to sit and slowly opened the white envelope.

Inside was a thin, faded-blue piece of paper that was folded into its own envelope, just like Divya Das's notes to Christian Hastings.

He must have wanted to return the note that he took that night they fought in her dorm room. She was about to shove the note in her bag when she noticed the black ink.

Divya Das always wrote in blue ink.

Glancing up at the front of the room one more time, she slipped the note out of the white envelope and opened it up. Her fingers began to tremble as she read the letter.

May 20, 1972
My life,
I don't accept.

> *I don't accept your need to sever your life from mine.*
>
> *I don't accept your excuses, your fear, or your paltry reasons for making other people happy while sacrificing your own happiness.*
>
> *I don't accept that we are so different that we can't overcome the barriers that society has erected in front of us.*
>
> *Yes, we will have higher mountains to climb, bigger hurdles to jump, and harder times ahead of us than most. But that doesn't mean that we can't do it. I know that you're scared because Vaneeta told your family about what she saw in the kaleidoscope room. I know you're frightened because your father and your mother may do something to cut you off from the only family that you know. I'm scared, too, because my family would do the same.*
>
> *But they underestimate us. They underestimate how strong we are together, how resilient we can be. And one day, I know they'll see that they were wrong, and they'll ask for our forgiveness.*

I love you, Divya, more than I've loved anyone or anything in my life. I know that you're the only one for me and that you will be the only one for me for as long as I live. From the first moment we met, our first conversation that lasted for hours, I was blessed to find the other half of my heart. I can't be the greatest person I will ever be in this world if I'm not complete. I know that deep down you also realize you can never be the Divya Das you've always dreamed of being if you're not free to love me, too.

I'm hoping you'll agree to take the jump with me. Tomorrow night, we'll meet in the kaleidoscope room. We'll open up the back exit, and we'll create a diversion so that your cousin will be too distracted to look for you on campus. It'll be a small one that can give us the time we need to disappear. I haven't figured out what it is yet, but I will before we meet. We'll burn our letters, and we'll ask our friends for help. My sister, Lydia, can help us get from Davidson Tower to the train station.

I've written to my grandmother in Charleston. She's willing to let us live with her. At least until we're on our feet. And since she doesn't talk to my father or my mother anymore, we'll be safe.

Meet me tomorrow at 8:00 p.m. Pack a small bag, and bring all your letters. No evidence will be left behind.

I love you, Divya. Your presence has been a fire in my heart and has ignited my soul. I want to spend the rest of my life cherishing you for bringing meaning to mine.

Your Jaan,
Christian Hastings

"Ms. Ahuja?"

Jessie looked up and realized that the class was staring at her. This time because Professor Barnard was in the front of the room, calling her name.

"I'm sorry, Professor Barnard," she said as she folded the letter and tucked it back in the folder. She cleared her voice from tears. It was easy to do now that she was filled with so much hope.

"Care to share with the class what was so exciting that you ignored the first two times that I called your name?"

There was a flutter of laughter from behind her. That didn't matter. None of them mattered. Jessie looked over her shoulder and met Ravi's eyes.

"I was actually reading some new evidence that I found for my paper. About Davidson Tower and the fire. Apparently, someone left the tower and slipped into a car right before the fire started."

Jessie didn't like making people feel uncomfortable, but in the moment, watching Professor Barnard's face blanch validated every moment that she and Ravi had spent looking through all those letters. The sound of students whispering to each other spread like a ripple across the room.

"That's fascinating," she said, and cleared her throat. She adjusted her suit coat like she always did at the beginning of a lecture. "I look forward to reading your paper, Ms. Ahuja."

Jessie nodded, then turned back to look at Ravi one last time.

Love you, he mouthed.

She smiled and turned in her seat so she could pay attention to the start of class.

TWENTY-SIX

Ravi

Ravi debated whether or not he should have written a letter from his own perspective instead of just giving her the letter from Christian, but in the end, there was so much meaning attached to Divya and Christian's story that it was better than any words that he could have come up with himself. It was what brought them together; it was what helped them fall in love and work as a team.

He waited patiently for class to end before he walked down the steps to her row. She stood, excitement in her eyes.

"How did you find it?"

"My brother helped me, actually," he said. He looked over at Professor Barnard, who was hastily gathering her things. "We went back to the tower," he said, lowering his voice. "We used Deep's keys to get in; then we opened that box of books you found. It was right on top. The same edition of *Persuasion* where we found Divya's letters."

Her eyes went wide. Then she smacked her palm against her forehead. "I should have made the connection, but I didn't realize! The books are *exactly* the same."

"Here's the thing," Ravi said as he took her backpack from her like he'd done for the last few weeks and slung it over his shoulder. "It was sitting right on top. There's no way someone didn't open that book and see those letters. I feel like they were meant to be found."

They both looked to the front of the classroom, where Professor Barnard had escaped. Ravi knew it had to be her.

He held Jessie's hand as they walked downstairs to the ground floor then out of the building.

"Are there more letters?" she asked, her excitement evident. "Did Christian have a stack?"

Ravi nodded. "I organized them in chronological order, then read the very last one." He pointed to the envelope she was holding. "I saved the rest of them so I could read them with you. Because we started this together, and I think we should end it together."

She grew quiet as they strolled towards the library. The air was cold now. Even though she was wearing a coat, the wind whipped through her hair and turned her cheeks pink.

Ravi wanted to pull her closer so that he could shield her from the wind. He'd done it before, and he hoped that in the future they'd have countless opportunities to do it again.

"Jessie."

"Ravi."

They spoke in unison, and then laughed.

Ravi looked around and realized they were standing smack dab in the middle of the university lawn. Across the way was the science building with the hidden terrace where Divya and Christian had their first date.

The lawn was mostly empty because of the weather, but that didn't matter. It was still the most visible point on campus.

"I love you," he said clearly. His voice carried. "I love you the way that Christian loved Divya and she loved him. I didn't at first when we met and you made me feel like I had to quit smoking and that I should feel grateful for having been born a Kumar. I did when you stood up to my father when no one else ever has. I'm strong enough to accept that I need to make decisions without worrying about what other people want me to be. Because what's the point in being a nepo baby if I don't take the opportunity to find my own way?"

She chuckled, then her eyes watered. "I didn't love you at first when you demanded my study room after you knew how much seeing the kaleidoscope room meant to me. But then you followed me home," she said quietly.

"Then I followed you home," he repeated. He dropped their backpacks to the ground between them, then held her hands together, warming them between his. "You asked me questions about what I wanted to do and who I wanted to be. You liked the same movies that I did, and you laughed at my jokes, and I think yours are hilarious even though you don't always realize it. I fell in love with you the first time we kissed."

Her tears spilled over, dampening her lashes until they glimmered. Her lower lip trembled, and she bit down on it, as if trying to keep her emotions under control. "Ravi," she said softly.

"I know you said you don't want to see me anymore, and if that's still true, I'll respect your boundaries. But I hope you see that we're stronger together than apart."

Shit, his voice was cracking. He thought he'd have the strength to get through this, but seeing the tears in her eyes made him feel so helpless. He cleared his throat.

"That's a pretty speech," she said, her tears falling freely.

"I'm a writer."

Her lips trembled into a tentative smile. "Will you promise to never make me feel like I'm not good enough or I'm less than the people in the world that you grew up in?"

"I will do my best, and I swear to god if I ever screw up, I'll do everything in my power to make it right."

Her hands curled over his, and he could feel the tiny, cracked shards of his heart start to gel together. He was finally able to take a deep breath.

"Did your brother make a call to my father out of pity, or to control him in some way?"

Ravi was already shaking his head. "In all the time that I've known you, I've realized one thing. Your goal in college is to prepare for a career that will let you give your parents the life you think they deserve. We're a team now, so I'm going to do what I can to help you give them that life, too."

Ravi heard the muffled sound of conversation behind them and knew that people were watching. He didn't care. He still hadn't gotten the answer he was hoping for. He'd wait for as long as he needed.

"I know that I've been judgmental and unfair to you," Jessie said. "And I realize I've been such a coward, making decisions about what-ifs instead of focusing on what we can control. But I promise that I've spent the last four days thinking about you, and I'm going to try just as hard as you will. I'm probably going to make mistakes, but like Christian and Divya, I think we'll be stronger together."

Ravi leaned in, gently resting his forehead against hers, a move that he'd done so many times now when he was feeling overwhelmed and just needed her peace. "Do you love me, Jessie Ahuja?"

"Yes," she said, her voice as clear and crisp as the winter wind. "I love you, even though I know that when your parents came and your brother showed up, you probably smoked with them."

He laughed. "It won't be a habit."

He let go of her hands and wrapped her up close, fitting her body against his. There was hollering from the background, cheering and clapping as if they were putting on a show.

It didn't matter. No one else mattered.

After one last kiss, he picked up their backpacks, linked her hand with his, and started in the direction of the library. "Come on," he said. "I'm going to buy you a latte, then take you to our study room. We have a paper to write."

"Then?" she said.

He let out a deep breath. "Then we do what Christian and Divya tried to do all those years ago. We live our lives. You'll take me on study dates to get truffle fries, and I'll drag you away from your books to go to parties. We'll practice your interviewing skills, and we'll convince my brother, who has been shitty to me all these years, to have his HR department give you an interview. If you're okay with a little helping hand and nepotism that is."

Her eyes were shining. "I don't know if I want to work for your brother after meeting him, to be honest, but I appreciate the offer."

"Always," he said.

"Ravi, I feel like this all sounds pretty anticlimactic compared to Divya and Christian, don't you think?"

"It sounds perfect," he said, and he squeezed her hand as they headed up the walkway to Hartceller Library. "Just having moments with you, living with you, Jessie, is a dream worth fighting for."

EPILOGUE

J essie placed the final box down in the guest room in Ravi's condo. Her car was now empty, and the chaos of the day had left her covered in a sheen of sweat. After hours trying to manage the move from Texas to New Jersey, she looked around at her mess: the half-packed boxes of clothes, the IKEA table and dresser boxes she'd recently purchased, the random suitcases filled with books and whatever else she had to shove into every nook and cranny of space she had.

The sound of the door opening led her back to the hallway to see if Ravi had returned.

"Hey!" she said when she saw him stroll in with Deep and Sahdna.

"Jessie!" Deep said, arms wide. He stopped when she held up her hands.

"I am a sweaty mess, Deep. You do not want to hug me."

He closed the space between them, wrapped his arms around her, and lifted her off her feet. "Yes, I do!" he said in a singsong voice. "It's good to see you after such a long summer."

She smiled. He'd grown on her now that she knew how to handle his energy. He was like a big teddy bear.

"I'll take a sweaty hug, too," Sahdna said from behind him. Jessie turned, and Sahdna squeezed her like they'd been apart for three years instead of three months. "It's good to see you."

"You, too," Jessie said. Feeling relieved to have Sahdna in her life. She was so honest all the time and had been one of the best confidantes as she and Ravi learned more about each other's worlds. "Are you going to come over for dinner as often as possible?"

Sahdna squeezed Jessie's hands. Her eyes sparkled. "I wouldn't have it any other way."

Jessie grinned. "I'll hold you to it."

Deep draped an arm over Sahdna's shoulder. "I can't believe that you and Ravi fell for first-year fresh meat."

Jessie looked up to see Ravi watching them, wearing a crooked smile. "I parked your car in the garage," he said.

"Thank you," she replied even as warmth pooled in her stomach at the sight of him.

Their relationship hadn't been easy. Between vacation breaks and a second semester where he had made a deal to intern part-time in the communications division of his father's company in exchange for access to the rest of his trust fund, they fought a lot. But they also took the time to talk it through. Most often, Ravi was the one writing her letters.

Jessie didn't know if she would ever get over being scared, but he was worth every moment of the fear. She was going to continue to brave an unknown future, because he was worth it. When Ravi had asked her to move in with him for his senior year and the subsequent two years of grad school he planned on completing at the university, she immediately said yes.

Then when school finished and he returned to working on his novel, they'd figure out what to do after that.

She saw the sparkle in his eye and knew he was about to kiss her. She braced herself when her phone rang.

Jessie patted her pockets, then held up a finger before she turned to jog back down the hallway to the guest bedroom where she was storing her things. She heard the ring again and saw the glittery case on top of an open box.

"Hello," she said breathlessly as she answered. The number was unknown, but given that it was the start of the semester, she was a little nervous about her scholarship aid. She picked up every call just in case it was the provost's office.

"Hello, is this Jessie Ahuja?" A kind voice, barely accented, spoke softly into the receiver.

"This is she," Jessie said. Her heart pounded, fear and hope twining in her heart.

"I'm so sorry that it's taken me so long to call you," the woman replied. "My sister-in-law passed on your information and your paper from her class last year. I haven't responded because I was first concerned about my privacy, and then I was traveling with my grandchildren."

Jessie's breath caught.

After she handed in her paper, she'd asked Professor Barnard to please share her number with Divya Das if they were still in touch, because she'd love to return her and Christian's letters.

She looked up just as Ravi stepped into the room. His brow furrowed. *Who is it?* he mouthed.

Jessie swallowed, then spoke into the phone, hoping with all her heart. "D-Divya Das?"

Ravi's eyes went wide. He wrapped his arms around her waist, pressing her flush against him so he could hear the conversation clearly.

The woman on the other end of the phone chuckled. "It's been Divya Hastings for some time now. I heard you have my letters. I'd love to see them again."

DEAR READER

I've always wanted to write a romance about letters. Maybe it was because I loved the old Bollywood movies where the hero and heroine stood in an archway and a sari fluttered in the wind while their eyes connected and their only method of communication was covertly written messages. Or maybe it was because I also loved *Pride and Prejudice* and the infamous Darcy letter.

Needless to say, letters have always been fascinating to me. But it wasn't until I was going through my grandmother's paperwork to close out her estate for my family that I realized how powerful letters could be. In the old cardboard boxes filled with a mishmash of medical bills and old naturalization paperwork, I found my grandmother's letters. She kept every single one she received. The most powerful letters were from her mother, whom she could never see again after she left India and moved to the United States.

It took me weeks to figure out what the letters said. They were all in Punjabi and Hindi, languages I can speak to some level of proficiency, but not read. But thanks to Google Translate, in the faded-blue pages still stamped with dates from the 1970s, I found hope and fear, happiness and sadness, and the truth about what my grandmother sacrificed to find opportunity in a foreign country. That was the genesis of this novel. And because my grandmother wrestled with her expectations versus her wants and needs, that's what I wanted to write about.

I work really hard to stay away from South Asian stereotypes about the Desi diaspora, or at the very least, I try to give meaning and nuance to age-old assumptions about South Asians. This book may feel like there are more stereotypes than most: hero who wants to write books instead of getting a job in tech, heroine who comes from a different socioeconomic class and does what her parents always wanted her to do.

Star-crossed lovers versus suitable arranged matches.

Whether you're Desi or not, it may sound familiar.

Here's the thing about stereotypes: Sometimes there is truth in them. And sometimes, that truth exists in privileged classes and communities the most because they are the ones resistant to change that may impact their same privilege. With Ravi and Jessie, you'll find that resistance, and you'll also see how both of them are very aware of their circumstances and the realities they can't escape.

But here's the good news! Because I write romances, and this book is indeed a romance novel, there is *always* a way out. There is always a path to happily ever after. There is always the slow unpacking of intergenerational trauma, addressing privilege and class, and the importance of standing up against cultural expectations.

And last but not least, there is always more to the story.

I hope you enjoy my first new-adult romance, friends. Ravi and Jessie are special to me, and I know they'll become just as special to you, too.

Trigger Warning in *The Letters We Keep*:
Vaping, which happens throughout the book

ACKNOWLEDGMENTS

I am always so afraid of writing acknowledgments because I know that there is a good chance I'm going to forget someone super important. So if you don't see your name here and you're a part of my life, just know that I still think you're a magical unicorn!

First, thank you to Carmen, Ronit, and the Skyscape team for always being so patient with me and encouraging me while I work through my messy, chaotic process.

Thank you to my partner in crime, Joy Tutela. The best wing woman in the industry!

Thanks to my besties: Jordan and Smita. And to my fam: my parents, Shikha, and Shiv.

To my hubs, who deserves the biggest, sloppy, smooching thank-you ever for putting up with my bullshit while I panicked and figured out how to send this story while we were supposed to be on vacation and spending time with each other.

To Sanjana Basker for the incredible notes, and to my sensitivity readers. Thank you for making this story so much better than I ever could on my own.

And thank you to my readers for always being so encouraging and loving and appreciative. You are the reason why I have this career, and I am forever grateful that I can write stories for you!

ABOUT THE AUTHOR

Photo © 2022 Marco Calerdon

Nisha Sharma is the award-winning author of *The Karma Map, Dating Dr. Dil,* and other adult contemporary and YA romances. Her books have appeared in best-of lists by the *New York Times,* the *Washington Post,* NPR, *Cosmopolitan, Teen Vogue,* Buzzfeed, and more. Nisha lives in Pennsylvania with her Alaskan husband; her cat, Lizzie Bennett; and her dogs, Nancey Drew and Madeline. For more information, visit www.nisha-sharma.com.